IRISH HIS´
AND
THE IRISH QU

GW00870406

BY
GOLDWIN SMITH

A long summer was spent by me in that loveliest of all parks, the Phœnix, as the guest of Edward Cardwell, then Chief Secretary and real head of the Irish government. Under Cardwell's roof the Irish Question was fully discussed by able men, Robert Lowe among the number. But I had a still greater advantage in constant and lasting intercourse with such friends as Lord Chancellor O'Hagan, Sir Alexander Macdonald, the head of the Education Department, and other leading Irish Liberals of the moderate school, ardent patriots and thoroughgoing reformers though opposed to violence and disruption. To the teachings of these men in dealing with the Irish Question, I have always looked back for my best guidance. I did what I could generally to acquaint myself with the country and its people. I had the opportunity of seeing something of Maynooth as the guest of its excellent principal in that day. At that time there was rather a lull in the agrarian war, but religious antagonism was still marked. The fruit of my[Pg iv] studies was a little book entitled "Irish History and Irish Character," in which I tried to show that the sources of Ireland's sorrows were to be found in natural circumstance and historical accident as much as in the crimes or follies of man in recent times. Upon that text I preached in favour of charity and reconciliation. I am told that a chord was touched at the time. But my essay has long been superseded and buried out of sight by the important works, historical and political, which the controversy has since produced, as well as by the forty eventful years which have elapsed since its publication. The subject, however, has retained all its interest, and my confidence in the wisdom of my Irish friends and instructors has remained the same, or rather has been strengthened by the course of events.

I was in Ireland again a good many years afterwards in connection with the meeting of the Social Science Association, and was the guest of Lord O'Hagan. The Parnellite Movement was then in full activity; American Fenianism was at work; and the soil heaved with insurrection. My friend W. E. Forster was the Secretary, and, much against his own inclination, was administering measures of repression, the only alternative to which[Pg v] appeared to be the abdication of the government. On this occasion I was unlucky enough to draw upon myself a thunderbolt hurled through the *Times*, but evidently from the skies, by hinting in a public speech that the Phœnix Park was as worthy to be the occasional residence of royalty as Osborne or Balmoral. A happy change, attended apparently with the best effects, has now come in that august quarter.

It is needless to say that this essay does not pretend to be a history of Ireland. It is an attempt to trace the general course of the history as it leads up to the present situation.

The works published in recent years to which I have been chiefly indebted are: Joyce's "Social History of Ancient Ireland," Richie's "Short History of the Irish People," Bagwell's "Ireland under the Tudors," Froude's "The English in Ireland," Lecky's "Leaders of Public Opinion in Ireland," together with the special chapters on Ireland in his general history, Ingram's "Two Chapters of Irish History" and "History of the Irish Union," Ball's "Irish Legislative Systems," T. P. O'Connor's "The Parnell Movement," and Sir Horace Plunkett's "Ireland in the Twentieth Century," with the comments on it by Father O'Riordan.

[Pg vi]To Mr. Bagwell's "Ireland under the Tudors" I am specially indebted for his narrative of the Tudor wars. To Mr. T. P. O'Connor I am specially indebted for the most vivid accounts of the famine and of the evictions, as well as for an improved insight into the Parnell Movement and of the doings which preceded it. Of part of those doings I was myself in some measure a witness, through my social connections with a circle of English politicians who were inclining to an Irish alliance.

The annals of the Tudor wars are horrible and heartrending. But history cannot drop the veil over them. They long left their evil traces on Irish character and sentiment, explaining and extenuating some terrible things which ensued. Nor, in truth, have they become obsolete as warnings to us in general of the acts into which civilized nations may be betrayed when they make wars of conquest on those whom they deem barbarians.

It seemed that a brief account of the recent land legislation for Ireland might be useful to readers of an essay of this kind. I append one which has been prepared for me by my friend, Mr. Hugh J. McCann, B.L., of the Dublin Bar. Its author is in no way committed to any opinion expressed in the other part of the work.

IRISH HISTORY AND THE IRISH QUESTION

I

Of all histories the history of Ireland is the saddest. For nearly seven centuries it was a course of strife between races, bloodshed, massacre, misgovernment, civil war, oppression, and misery. Hardly even now have the troubles of Ireland come to a close, either for herself or for her partner. Unrest still reigns in her and, embodied in her Parliamentary delegation, harasses the Parliament and distracts the councils of Great Britain.

The theatre of this tragedy is a large island lying beside one nearly three times larger, which cuts it off from the continent of Europe, while on the other side it fronts the wide ocean. The climate is for the most part too wet for wheat. The pasture is very rich. Ireland seems by nature to be a grazing country, and a country of large farms; tillage and small farms have been enforced by the redundance of rural population consequent on the destruction[Pg 2] of urban industries. In coal and minerals Ireland is poor, while the sister island abounds in them, and in its swarming factories and mines furnishes a first-rate market for the produce of Irish pastures; so that the two islands are commercial supplements of each other. The progress of pastoral countries, political and general, as they have little city life, is slow. With beauty Ireland is well endowed. The interior is flat, with large peat bogs and brimming rivers. But the coast is mountainous and romantic. The western coast especially, where the Atlantic rolls into deep inlets, has a pensive charm which, when troubles end and settled peace reigns, may attract the villa as they do the wanderer now. In early times the island was densely clothed with woods, which, with the broad and bridgeless rivers, operated like the mountain barriers of the Scottish Highlands in perpetuating the division of clans, with their patriarchal system, their rivalries, and their feuds, thus precluding the growth of a nation. In Ireland there was no natural centre of dominion. Interest of every kind seems to enjoin the union of the islands. But in the age of conquest the weaker island was pretty sure to be marked as a prey of the stronger, while the difficulties of access, the Channel, broad in the days of primitive navigation,[Pg 3] and the Welsh mountains, combined with the internal barriers of forest and river and with the naturally wild habits of the people, portended that the conquest would be difficult and that the agony would be long. Such was the mould of Destiny.

The people of Ireland when history opens were Celts, kinsmen of the primitive races of Gaul and Britain, remnants of which are left in Wales and in the Highlands of Scotland. Their language was of that family, while cognate words connect it with the general Aryan stock. There are traces of a succession of immigrations. Too much, no doubt, has been made of the influence of race. Yet the Teuton is a Teuton and the Celt is a Celt. The Celt in his native state has everywhere shown himself lively, social, communicative, impulsive, prone to laughter and to tears, wanting, compared with the Teuton, in depth of character, in steadiness and perseverance. He is inclined rather to personal rule or leadership than to a constitutional polity. His poet is not Shakespeare or Milton, but Tom Moore, a light minstrel of laughter and tears. His political leader is O'Connell, a Boanerges of passionate declamation. In war he is impetuous, as was the Gaul who charged at Allia and the Highlander who charged at Killiecrankie and Prestonpans.[Pg 4] His taste as well as his manual skill in decoration is shown by the brilliant collection of gold ornaments in the Celtic Museum at Dublin, as well as in stone carvings and such a paragon of illuminated missals as the Book of Kells. But it is greater than his aptitude for high art, that art which treats the human form, in which he has not shone. His religious tendency, the outcome of his general character, is either to Catholicism with its fervid faith, its mysteries, and its ceremonial, as in Ireland; or to the enthusiastic forms of Protestantism, as in the Highlands and in Wales. Anglicanism, a sober cult with a balanced creed, suits him not. It was a cruel decree of destiny that the larger island from which the conqueror would come was peopled by the Teuton, so that to the usual evils of conquest was added that of a difference of character inherent in race.

The primitive organization of the Irish Celts was tribal, the underlying idea being kinship, real or reputed. The ruler with paternal authority was the chief of the tribe. To avert strife his tanist, or successor, was elected in his lifetime. In a community of reputed kinsmen there could be no aristocracy of birth; but there seems to have been a plutocracy, whose riches in that pastoral country[Pg 5] consisted of cattle, which formed the measure of wealth and command of which made poorer clansmen their retainers. Under these were the freemen of the tribe. Under the freemen again were the unfree, wanderers or captives taken in war or slaves from the English slave-market. The unfree appear to have been the only tillers of the soil. Thus tillage was marked with a bar sinister from its birth. The tribal law was a mystical and largely fanciful craft or tradition in the keeping of the Brehons, or judges, a hereditary order who, though revered as arbiters, were without power of enforcing their judgments. Like primitive law in general, it lacked the idea of public wrong. It treated crime as a private injury, to be compounded by fine. The land was the common property of the tribe, to which it nominally reverted on the demise of the holder, though it may be assumed that the chiefs at all events had practically land of their own and that the tendency in this, as in other cases, was to private ownership.

What the religion was is not certainly known. Probably it was the same as that of the Celts of Great Britain and Gaul, Druidism, wild, orgiastic, and perhaps sanguinary. But there seem to be no remains clearly Druidic in Ireland.

[Pg 6]Life was pastoral, roving, probably bellicose. It appears that women required to be restrained from taking part in war. The characteristic garb of the tribesman was a loose saffron mantle, which served as his dress by day, his coverlet by night. His favourite weapons, often used, were an axe and a dart. He drew, it seems, a bow weak compared with the long-bow of England. The gentler side of his character was shown in his passionate love of the harp and the reverence in which he held the harper, and which was extended to the bard, whose rude lays saluted the intellectual dawn and whom we find in later times feared as an author of lampoons. Among his favourite amusements was chess.

Knowledge of the peculiar system of the Irish, political and legal, is of more consequence because the opposite system, that of constitutional government and feudal ownership, having presented itself to him as that of alien masters and oppressors, tribal peculiarities and sentiments lingered long. The idea of tribal ownership perhaps a few generations ago still faintly present in agrarian agitation. Nor has the general character of the tribesman long been, if it yet is, extinct. Tribal feuds were until lately represented in the strange faction fights of the Caravats and Shanavests, the[Pg 7] Two-Year-Olds and Three-Year-Olds, the annual fight of factions for a legendary stone, and the encounters between bodies of the peasantry at Irish fairs. Perhaps another feature of character traceable to tribalism may be the gregarious habit of Irishmen contrasted with the Englishman's isolation and love of his private home.

Connected apparently with the tribal sentiment were the strange customs of fosterage and gossipred. Fosterage consisted in putting out the child to be reared by a tribesman who became its foster-father. Gossipred, a Christian addition, was a spiritual kinship formed at the font. Both relations had extraordinary force.

There were, of course, tribal wars. There were leagues or dominations of powerful tribes which left their traces in the division of the island into four or five provinces, once petty kingships. There was a supreme kingship, the seat of which, sacred in Irish tradition and legend, was the Hill of Tara; but it was probably only when common danger compelled a union of forces that this kingship became a real power. The features of the country, combined with the character of the tribal organization based on kinship, not on citizenship, would prolong the tribal divisions and prevent union. Nor[Pg 8] had nature anywhere fixed a central seat of command. Only when opposed to an invader and struggling against him for the land did Celtic Ireland form for the time a united people; even then it could hardly be called a nation.

The Roman conqueror looked, but came not. It might have been better for Ireland if he had come. Yet, when he retired, he would probably have left the Romanized provincial, here as in Britain, too unwarlike to hold his own against the next invader.

A conqueror of a different kind came. He came in the person, not of a Roman general, but, if the tradition is true, of a slave. By the preaching of St. Patrick, according to the common belief, Ireland was added to the Kingdom of Christ. The conversion was rapid and probably superficial, the chief of the tribe carrying the tribe over with him, as Ethelbert of Kent and other English kinglets carried over their people, rather to a new religious allegiance than to a new faith.

Within the Roman Empire the centres of the Church had been the cities. Cities were the seats of its bishoprics. The models of its organization were urban. But in Ireland there were no cities. The episcopate was irregular and weak, denoting rank rather than authority or jurisdiction. The[Pg 9] life of the Church was monastic and missionary. The weird Round Towers, believed to have been places of refuge for its ministers and their sacred vessels, as well as bell-towers, speak of a life surrounded by barbarism and rapine as well as threatened by the heathen and devastating Northmen. Partly perhaps owing to its comparative isolation and detachment at home, the Irish clergy was fired with a marvellous and almost preternatural zeal for the propagation of the Gospel abroad. It crossed the sea to Iona, the sacred isle, still to religious memory sacred, from which the light of the Gospel shone to the wild islesmen and to the rovers of the Northern Sea. Irish missionaries preached to heathen Germany, colliding there, it seems, with a more regular episcopate. They played a part in the conversion of Britain not less important than that of the missionaries of Rome, before whose authority, however, the Irish Church in the person of Aidan was at last compelled to retire, the decisive struggle taking place on the mode of celebrating Easter.

In Ireland itself there arose in connection with the Church a precocious and romantic passion for learning which founded primitive universities. Its memory lingers in the melancholy ruins of [Pg 10]Clonmacnoise. This was the delusive brightness of a brief day, to be followed by the darkness of a long night.

The Church of Ireland seems in its origin to have been national and neither child nor vassal of Rome. Its theology must have been independent if Scotus Erigena was its son. But Rome gradually cast her spell, in time she extended her authority, over it. Its heads looked to her as the central support of the interests of their order and as their protectress against the rude encroachments of the native chiefs. Norman Archbishops of Canterbury served as transmitters of the influence. Still, the Irish Church was not in Roman eyes perfectly regular. Tithes were not paid, nor was the rule of consanguinity observed, or the rite of baptism administered in strict accordance with the ordinances of Rome.

Christianity did not kill the brood of a lively superstition, the fairy, the banshee, the spectre, charms, amulets, prophecies, wild legends, which in the times of gloom that followed strengthened their hold upon Irish imagination.

Hostile invasion came first in the form of the Northmen, whose piracy and rapine extended to Ireland as well as to Gaul and Britain. Piracy and rapine we call them now, but to the Northmen[Pg 11]they seemed no more criminal than to us seems hunting or fishing. The chief objects of the invader's attack were the monasteries, at once treasuries of Church wealth and hateful to the people of Odin. Ruthlessly the Northman slew and burned. His fleet made him ubiquitous and baffled defence, union for which there was not at first among the tribes. Common danger at last enforced it. A national leader arose in the person of Brian Boru, who was for Ireland the military, though not the political, saviour that Alfred was for England. At the great battle of Clontarf, the host over which the Danish Raven flew was totally overthrown, and Ireland was redeemed from its ravages. The Dane, however, did not wholly depart. Exchanging the rover for the trader, he founded a set of little maritime commonwealths at Dublin, Wexford, Waterford, and Limerick, germs on a small scale and in a rude way of municipal as well as commercial life.

But a conqueror, more fell and more tenacious than the Dane, was at hand. In 1169 a little fleet of Welsh vessels ran into the Bay of Bannow. From it landed a band of mail-clad soldiery, men trained to war, with a corps of archers. They were Normans from Wales under the leadership of the[Pg 12] Anglo-Norman rover Fitzstephen, and were the precursors of a larger body which presently followed, under Richard Strigul, Earl of Pembroke, from the strength of his arm surnamed Strongbow. Dermot, an Irish chief, expelled for his tyranny, had brought these invaders on his country as the instruments of his revenge. Henry II. had, by giving letters of marque, sanctioned the enterprise, the fruits of which he intended to reap. Early in his reign the king had obtained from Pope Adrian IV., an Englishman by birth, a bull authorizing him to take possession of Ireland, which with other islands the bull declared of right to be an appanage of the Holy See. Here, as in the case of William's invasion of England, the Papacy used Norman conquest as the instrument of its own aggrandizement. The authenticity of the bull is disputed by Irish patriotism, but in vain. No one questions the share of the Papacy in the Norman conquest of England.

With the aid of his Norman allies, to whom the Irishman with his naked valour was as the Mexican to the Spaniard, Dermot prevailed and glutted his revenge by plucking from the triumphal pyramid of hostile heads that of his chief enemy and tearing it with his teeth. But in this case, as in that of the alliance of Cortez with the Tlascalans, the ally had[Pg 13] conquered for himself. Declining to be dislodged, he proceeded to establish himself and to organize a Norman principality.

Now the jealousy of the English king was aroused. He saw an independent Anglo-Norman kingdom on the point of being founded by Strongbow in Ireland. He published the papal bull, came over to Ireland in his power, and held his court at Dublin in a palace of wickerwork run up in native style for the occasion, where the Irish chiefs bowed their heads, but not their hearts, before him. He organized a feudal principality with himself as lord, but having the Pope as its suzerain, and tributary to the Papacy. He formally introduced the organization of a feudal kingdom. He held at Cashel a synod like that held by William the Conqueror at Winchester for the purpose of reforming, that is thoroughly Romanizing, the Church of Ireland. Irregularities respecting infant baptism and the matrimonial table of consanguinity were set right. The payment of tithes, that paramount duty of piety, was enjoined. Rome was installed in full authority, thus in Ireland, as in England, receiving from her Norman liegemen her share of their prize. With this pious offering to the Papacy in his hand, Henry departed to meet his responsibility for the slaying[Pg 14] of Becket. He was presently succeeded for a short time in Ireland by his hopeful boy, John, whose personal behaviour was an earnest of the future tenour of his reign. Afterward, as king, John paid Ireland another flying visit in which, besides pouncing on an enemy, he seems to have made a fleeting attempt to regulate the government.

Henry, had he not been called away by the storm following the death of Becket, might have left things in better shape, but nothing could make up for the permanent absence of the

4

king. Two antagonistic systems henceforth confronted each other. On one side was the feudal system, with its hierarchy of land-owners, from lord-paramount to tenant-paravail; its individual ownership of land; its hereditary succession and primogeniture; its feudal perquisites, relief, wardship, and marriage; its tribute of military service; the loyalty to the grantor of the fief which was its pervading and sustaining spirit; its knighthood and its chivalry; its Great Council of barons and baronial bishops; its feudal courts of justice and officers of state; all however highly rude and imperfect. On the other side was tribalism, with its tie of original kinship instead of territorial subordination; its tanistry; its Brehon law. But the feudal system in Ireland lacked the[Pg 15] keystone of its arch. It was destitute of its regulating and controlling power, the king. A royal justiciar could not fill the part. From the outset the bane of the principality was delegated rule.

Ireland was a separate realm, though attached to the Crown of England. It had a Parliament of its own, which followed that of England in its development, being at first a unicameral council of magnates, lay and clerical; but after the legislation of Edward I. a bicameral assembly with a Lower House formed of representatives of counties and boroughs, whose consent would be formally necessary to taxation. Representatives of Ireland were at first called to Edward's Parliament at Westminster, but the inconvenience seems to have been found too great. Weak, however, was the Parliament of the colony compared with that of the imperial country. If the Lords ever showed force, the making of a House of Commons was not there. The representation, as well as the proceedings and the records, appears to have been very irregular. Nothing worthy of the name of Parliamentary government seems ever to have prevailed. Among those who signed the Great Charter was the Archbishop of Dublin; but of chartered rights Ireland was not the scene. There is no appearance of a separate[Pg 16] grant of subsidies by the clerical estate. The clergy, it seems, were represented by their proctors in the Lower House, as by the bishops and abbots in the Upper House. The Parliament appears to have been generally a tool in the hands of the deputy. The irregularity of its composition seems to have extended to its meetings.

From the first the relation between the feudal realm and that of the tribes was border war. They were alien to each other in race, language, and social habits, as well as in political institutions. The Norman could not subdue the Celt, the Celt could not oust the Norman. The conquest of England by William of Normandy had been complete, and had given birth to a national aristocracy, which in time blended with the conquered race and united with it in extorting the Great Charter. The Norman colony in Ireland was left to its feeble resources, and to a divided command, while the monarchy was far away over sea, was squandering its forces in French fields, and could not even project a complete conquest. Besides, there were the difficulties which the country, with its broad rivers, its bogs, its mountains and forests, opposed to the heavy cavalry of the Anglo-Norman. There was the mobility of a pastoral people, presenting no cities[Pg 17] or centres of any kind for attack, driving its cattle to the woods on the approach of the invader, and eluding his pursuit like birds of the air. Thus the Anglo-Norman colony failed to become a dominion and presently dwindled to a pale. Between the Pale and the Celt incessant war was waged with the usual atrocity of struggles between the half-civilized and the savage. Fusion there could be none. There was not the bond of human brotherhood or that of a common tongue. On neither side was the murder of the other race a crime. Never was there a more inauspicious baptism of a nation.

Anglo-Norman and Celt, feudalist and tribesman, alike were Catholics. A common religion might have been a bond, a common clergy might have been a mediating power. But race and language prevailed over religion. The Churches, though outwardly of the same faith, remained inwardly separate, and not only separate but hostile to each other, the clergy on both sides sharing the spirit and the atrocities of race enmity and frontier war. The Church of the tribes was still very rough and irregular. The Norman on his part was devout. He was a founder of monasteries, thereby discharging his conscience of a load not seldom heavy. Whatever of religious life and activity there was in[Pg 18] the Pale seems to have been monastic. Our glimpses of the secular clergy show that they were secular indeed. Among them not neglect of duty only but criminality appears to have been rife.

In the little commercial towns of Danish foundation on the coast which had been taken over by the Norman, life was probably rather more civilized; but they were too diminutive to exert any influence beyond their gates. Galway in time became the port of an active trade with Spain which is supposed to have left a Spanish trace on its architecture and a Spanish strain in the blood of its people.

5

II

It was not likely that the colony, in the state in which it was, would gain by emigration from England. It was probably losing by depletion. English kings drew soldiers from it for their wars. There being no university or means of education, youths who wanted to study went to Oxford, where, though they were not native Irish, they seem to have played in academical brawls the part which native Irish might have played. Thus the colony was emptied of its intellect. Fiefs by feudal rule of descent passed to absentees and to women, weakening its military force. In every way the life-blood of the English and feudal settlement was being continually withdrawn. Of the kings of England, Richard I. was away on crusade, John and Henry III. were wrestling with rebellion at home. The thoughts of Edward I. were turned to Ireland; but his energies were absorbed by Scotland, Wales, and Gascony. He too drew soldiers from Ireland.

The Anglo-Norman element, however, was united, while inveterate disunion reigned among the native[Pg 20] tribes. It was occupying the posts of vantage with the castles characteristic of its military rule. It seems to have been rather gaining ground when the island was invaded by Edward Bruce, the brother of Robert, who, emulous of his brother's success in Scotland, came over on the invitation of Irish tribes to carve out a kingdom for himself. Bruce gained successes and committed great ravages, but was at length met at Dundalk by the Anglo-Norman army under John de Bermingham, overthrown, and slain. He had estranged his Irish allies. According to one of their chroniclers, the day on which he was slain was the happiest of days for the Irish people. The Irish appeal to the Pope against English misrule on this occasion is in form a national manifesto, but was probably less than national in its source.

Still Bruce's invasion seems to have dealt the Norman colony a heavy blow and thrown back into the hands of the native tribes districts which it had conquered and over which its settlements had spread. Degeneration set in amongst its people. They took to the strange native custom of fosterage, to the Irishman's saffron mantle and his long moustache, to his weapons, to his mode of riding, even to his language, and countenanced[Pg 21] license by confusing the Brehon with the feudal law.

A strange compound of feudalism with tribalism ensued, in the shape of mongrel chieftaincies, henceforth the predominant powers. English barons doffed their baronial character, donned that of the tribal chief, and made themselves independent lords of wide domains peopled by native Irish. It seems that they retained the Norman instinct of command. Many of them changed their Anglo-Norman for Irish names; Bourke, O'Neill, O'Brien, O'Connor. They kept in their pay troops of bravos, gallowglasses and kernes. Their rule seems to have combined the extortions of the feudal lord with those of the native chiefs. Bonaught was a tax imposed by a chief for the support of his mercenaries. Sorohen was an obligation on lands to support the chief with his train one day in a quarter or one in a fortnight. Coshery was a chief's right to sponge upon his vassals with as many followers as he pleased. Cuddies, or night suppers, were due by lands upon which the chief might quarter himself and his train for four days four times a year. Shragh and mart were yearly exactions in money and kine, apparently imposed at will. But worst of all was coyne[Pg 22] and livery, horse-meat and man-meat taken at will. This, it seems, was not an Irish but an Anglo-Norman invention introduced at first as the means of coping with Edward Bruce, but, like the income tax, perpetuated when the special need was past. The chiefs deemed themselves independent princes, renouncing openly or practically allegiance to the English Crown. It is with these potentates and the forces which their restless and rebellious ambition could command that the Crown henceforth in its struggle with the Irish difficulty has to deal. Had they been united, they might have prevailed; but they were always at feud with each other, while policy, though not loyalty, led some of them to side with the Crown. Of the septs, the three most powerful were the Geraldines of the north, close to Dublin, the head of which became afterward Earl of Kildare; the Geraldines of the south in Munster, the head of which became Earl of Desmond; and the Butlers, also in the south, whose head became the Earl of Ormonde. The O'Neills in Ulster were another powerful sept. The Butlers, less Hibernized than their rivals, were almost always on the side of the Crown.

To put a stop to degeneration and restore order in the Pale by the talismanic influence of royalty,[Pg 23] Edward III. sent over his son Lionel, Duke of Clarence. Under the duke's influence the Irish Parliament passed the statute of Kilkenny, drawing a sharp line of division between the two races; declaring marriage, fosterage, gossiped, and even concubinage with the Irish high treason; pronouncing the same penalties against supplying horses and armour to Irishmen or furnishing them with provisions in time of war; commanding Englishmen to speak English, to bear English names only, and to ride and dress in the English fashion; providing for the arming of the colony against Irish enemies; separating in every way the native Irishman from the Englishman and even forbidding the admission of Irish priests to livings in the English Church or to the English monasteries. There are severe regulations against the entertainment of Irish story-tellers and bards. An article declaring the English born in Ireland and in England to be equal and forbidding them to call each other English Hobbe or Irish Dog on pain of a year's imprisonment and a fine at the king's pleasure shows that there was a social division in the colony on that line. The statute betrays despair of a fusion of races or of a subjection of the whole island to English rule and law. At the same time it seems[Pg 24] to restrain English aggression and decree peace between the races.

Piqued, we are told, by a taunt of his impotence as lord of Ireland which stung his pride, Richard II. twice came over to Ireland with a large army. His armies were wrecked by the difficulties of the country and the passionate weakness of their commander. From his second visit Richard was recalled by the knell of his own doom.

The Pale was drawn into the troubles of the Roses. Before the outbreak the Duke of York had come over to Ireland as vicegerent, won the heart of the people, asserted the independence of the Irish Parliament, and seemed disposed to make himself king. He had been recalled by the Civil War, but he had left behind him a Yorkist party which adhered to the White Rose after Bosworth, recognized the two pretenders, Lambert Simnel and Perkin Warbeck, and fought for the lost cause by the side of Martin Schwartz and his German hackbut-men at Stoke.

The Anglo-Norman colony or "Pale" was now at its nadir. Much of its manhood had been drawn away by the kings to their Scottish and French wars. It was reduced to a circle of two counties and a half round Dublin, defended by a ditch. Had[Pg 25] the chiefs of tribes been unanimous, it would almost certainly have been destroyed. But the chiefs of tribes were very far from being unanimous, and thanks to their dissensions Strongbow in his tomb at Christ Church still slept undisturbed on the field of his victory. In the Pale itself reigned corruption, disorder, and misrule. "There is no land in all this world that has more liberty in vices than Ireland and less liberty in virtue." Such, as reported to Henry VIII., was the internal condition of the colony; and the description extended in its full force to the Church.

The hostility of the Pale to the Red Rose probably combined with distractions at home in leading Henry VII. to try the policy of winning the great Irish chiefs to allegiance by marks of confidence and honour and of governing Ireland through them. He tried it with the Earl of Kildare, the head of the great Geraldine clan, saying, as the story went, when he was told that all Ireland could not govern that man, "then that man shall govern all Ireland." Kildare, deported to England as a suspected traitor, but there winning favour and confidence by the artful address in which his kind were seldom wanting, was sent back to Ireland as lord deputy. The policy had a show of success.[Pg 26] Kildare as deputy harried the lands of his own enemies and reported execution done on the enemies of the Crown. He gained one signal victory of that kind. But the attempt to employ restless and lawless ambition as the regular mainstay of orderly government could not be a permanent success. The sept of Butler alone was true to the Crown. The next reign saw Kildare's son and successor as deputy in the Tower, and his grandson, Silken Thomas, raising a madcap rebellion which was made impious by the murder of an archbishop. The execution of Silken Thomas and his five uncles closed the experiment of governing Ireland through that house. There was left one boy whom faithful guardians carried abroad and to whom the heart of the sept still turned.

To make an end of the aspirations to independent nationality which had budded under the Duke of York, and bring Irish legislation completely under the control of the Crown, the Lord Deputy Poynings caused to be carried through the Parliament of the Pale the pair of acts which bore his name, subjecting Irish legislation to the control of the English Council. The first act ordained that in future no Parliament should be held in Ireland "but at such season as the King's [Pg 27]Lieutenant-in-Council there first do certify the King under the great seal of that land the causes and considerations, and all such acts as then seemeth should pass in the said Parliament." Should the king in council approve, the Irish Parliament was to be summoned under the great seal of England and not otherwise. The second act provided that all public statutes "late made within the realm of England" should be in force in Ireland. This it was decided applied to all English acts prior to the tenth year of Henry VII. Ireland was thus practically turned from a separate principality into a political dependency of England. The work of Poynings was long afterwards completed by the act of George I. affirming the right of the British Parliament to legislate for Ireland.

[Pg 28]

7

III

During the early part of the reign of Henry VIII. the policy of the English government was a continuation of that of Henry VII. It was a policy of conciliation and of ruling through the great Irish chiefs, the heads of the Butlers, the Geraldines, and the O'Neills, who were gratified by the bestowal of English titles of nobility, with flattering marks of confidence, and by a change in the tenure of their land from tribal to feudal, which invested them with full ownership. The Irish chief and the feudal baron of the Pale now sat in Parliament together for the first and last time. There appears to have been an inclination on the part of the Crown to favour the native Irish, it being still remembered perhaps that the Anglo-Irish had supported the Yorkist pretenders. The king himself penned a sage and benevolent manifesto, in the shape of a despatch to the Lord Deputy Surrey, on the blessings of civilization. The policy of conciliation was in fact necessary as well as laudable; for the king, plunged by his diplomacy[Pg 29] into continental embroilments and lavishing his father's hoard on a Field of the Cloth of Gold, had not the means of subduing Ireland. It would have been vain to look in those days for the philosophy which could make allowance for a diversity of national ideas and habits. The O'Neill, upon his elevation to the earldom of Tyrone, is required with his heirs to forsake the name of O'Neill, to use English habits and the English language. The age, however, was one of growing light. Education was a passion of the hour. A decree in favour of the establishment of a system of free schools in Ireland went forth. Unhappily it remained a decree. No homilies, no peerages, no flatteries or marks of confidence could permanently avail to quiet the intractable ambition of the great chiefs. They took the titles, which tickled their vanity; but they preferred the state of a chieftain with his gallowglasses and with his despotic power over the sept to that of a baron under royal rule, with feudal restraints and obligations. They were always at feud with each other, waging private war and ravaging each others' territories with the ruthlessness of the most cruel invader. Murders among them were frequent. Conspiracies were always on foot. Thus the catastrophe of the house[Pg 30] of Kildare ended what may be called the early Tudor policy of native government and conciliation. The policy of conquest with colonization in its train prevailed once more.

The instrument of that policy was to be a line of English deputies; able men on the whole and zealous in the public service, but generally incapable of understanding any national character or any institutions but their own. A deputy had also to contend with desperate difficulties, utter insufficiency of military force, an empty exchequer, a service full of jobbery and corruption, hostile intrigue both at Dublin and in the court at home.

The line was opened by Skeffington, a good though somewhat decrepit soldier, before whose artillery fell the redoubtable native fortress of Maynooth. The Crown had now a new and formidable force upon its side in the cannon, which it alone could afford to maintain. In Ireland as elsewhere the end of the feudal fortress had come.

At the same time there were forfeited to the Crown great tracts of land held by absentees, the feudal principle still prevailing and military service being still a condition of the ownership of land. The Crown thereby became a landowner on a vast scale, with the means of planting settlements in all the[Pg 31] districts under its power. Thus a wide field was opened for Crown colonization.

But now comes an event most momentous in itself and fraught with future woe to Ireland. Henry VIII., enraged at the refusal of the Pope to let him put away his wife and marry another woman, breaks with the Papacy, carries his kingdom out of its dominion, declares himself supreme head of a national Church, dissolves the monasteries, seizes their estates, and half reforms the church in a Protestant sense, breaking the worshipped images, closing the shrines, expurgating the liturgy, and licensing the translation of the Bible. He seizes into his own hands under the mask of a *congé d'élire* the appointments to the bishoprics. Wavering to the last in opinion between Catholicism and Protestantism according as the party of the old or that of the new aristocracy prevailed in his councils, he in the upshot practically ranges his kingdom on the Protestant side in the grand struggle that was to come between the Catholic and the Protestant powers.

In Ireland there was one religion but there were two Churches: that of the Pale and that of the native Irish; divided from each other, not by doctrine or ritual, but by race and language, practically treating[Pg 32] each other as not within the pale of Christendom, hardly within the pale of humanity. No Irishman could be admitted to church preferment or to a monastery in the Pale. Nor did the churches ever act together as one Church. Both were in a most miserable condition. The edifices were in ruins, the services were unperformed. Monasteries however abounded. They were the refuge of the peaceful in that world of strife and blood. That some of them were on a large scale stately ruins prove. It is surmised that they may have been wealthy, if not in lands, in orchards, fish-ponds, mills, or the labour which seems to have been sheltered within their ample walls. Like the English monasteries, they impropriated the tithes of parishes, thus helping to kill the parochial system. The character of the clergy was still scandalously low, not seldom criminal. Among the people religion was almost dead; the remnant of it, as well as the remnant of education, was kept alive by the poor Franciscan friars. In neither Church was there the making of martyrs.

In the little maritime towns there was more religion, as well as something more like civilization. But in this as in other respects their influence was confined to their own gates.

[Pg 33]There was no opposition in the Irish Parliament to the change of the king's title from *Dominus* to *Rex*, whereby the sovereignty of the Pope was cancelled, to any article in the king's assumption of autocratic power over the Church, or to his taking to himself the appointment of bishops. A show of resistance made by the proctors of the clergy in the House of Commons was promptly met by their extrusion. Nor was there the slightest unwillingness on the part of any lord or chief to take his share of the plunder of the monasteries, which, as in England, were suppressed, with confiscation of revenue and goods, including the impropriated tithes of parishes which they had served. A plea put in by the deputy on behalf of six friaries in consideration of their special services to education and their hospitality was not heard.

The iconoclastic part of the revolution, attacking the material objects of popular worship, relics, wonder-working images, and venerated shrines, seems to have encountered some natural resistance, and it appears that the government failed to put an end to pilgrimages, which were the religious pleasure-trips of the people.

The leader of the Reform movement, and specially of iconoclasm, in Ireland, under Henry VIII.,[Pg 34] was Archbishop Browne, a fervid but apparently not discreet man. He had a rather restive coadjutor in Bishop Staples. No counterpart of Cranmer, Latimer, or Ridley appeared.

The members of the council of Edward VI., being men of the new official aristocracy, opposed to the old houses, attached themselves to the party of movement in religion. In England they completed the work of confiscation, carried iconoclasm a step farther, and made Protestant reforms in the religious system, the last in conjunction with foreign reformers. Their policy in Ireland was the same. They sent over the prayer-book of Edward. But the effect appears to have been small. The way had not been prepared by the advent of Lutheranism or by the use of translations of the Bible. Besides, there was no religious feeling on which it could act. The Deputy St. Leger was a shrewd man of the world, who, while he was ready to put the law in force, disliked all religious agitation. "Tut, tut," he said to the earnest reformer, "your religious matters will spoil all." The way of the new liturgy was effectually blocked by the Erse language, and no missionary effort appears to have been made.

The military policy of Edward's government[Pg 35] had a very able though rather grim representative in Bellingham, if he had only been backed by a sufficient force. But the foreign complications of England being what they were, no sufficient force could ever be sent. The system of regular hostings against the natives is now on foot. Bellingham having stormed a position, there ensues a butchery of wood kerne, the equal of which Bellingham supposed there had never been. "Such," the deputy says, "was the great goodness of God to deliver them into our hands." Puritanism with its ruthlessness is making its appearance in the lists, on one side, while on the other side enters its mortal foe the Jesuit.

The government incurred deserved hatred in Ireland as in England by carrying to further lengths the debasement of the coin which had been the disgraceful shift of the spendthrift Henry VIII. A petition sent to the king upon the subject, in setting forth the folly of debasement, stated with an accuracy remarkable for the time the function of the precious metals as a medium of exchange. Wholesale fraud on the part of government was not likely to help the cause of the Reformation.

Beyond the English Pale the change of religion never reached the people. Antagonism of religion[Pg 36] was henceforth added to estrangement of race. Protestantism was to be the religion of the conqueror; Catholicism was to be the religion of the conquered. The Pope became a rival in sovereignty to the king of England, claiming the allegiance at once of piety and patriotism. Instead of the torpid clergy of the old native Church, now came upon the scene active emissaries of Rome with the Jesuit, master of intrigue, at their head, to do the joint work of propagandism and rebellion. Presently will appear the crusading soldiery of Catholic Spain.

With Mary comes an interlude of reaction. The sovereignty was not restored to the Pope. Grantees of abbey lands in Ireland, as in England, Catholics though they might be, held fast their prey. But the old ritual was for a time legally revived, and the hand of iconoclasm was stayed. Protestantism was rabbled; but Smithfield fires, the martyr's spirit being absent, there were none.

A story is told of an envoy sent by Mary to Ireland with a warrant of persecution, whose commission a clever Protestant woman, in whose house he put up by the way, stole and replaced

9

by a pack of cards, so that when the deputy opened the wallet at the council board nothing came forth but the pack of cards with the knave of clubs uppermost.

[Pg 37]

IV

Thus the day of the Elizabethan era which dawned so brightly upon England came on in heavy clouds for the unhappy dependency. The religious compromise which it brought to England was adapted by the English statesmen who framed it to the religious condition and temperament of their own people. To the condition and temperament of the Irish people there was no such adaptation. To the Catholic lords of the Pale the Elizabethan religion was alien; to the native Celts it was not only alien, but utterly abhorrent. It presented itself, not as the religion of Ireland, but as the religion of the conqueror.

The ecclesiastical polity comprised in the Act of Uniformity and the Thirty-nine Articles was, however, formally extended to Ireland, and the Crown resumed the powers which it had assumed in the time of Henry VIII. or his son, including the appointment of bishops, in this case without the veil, retained in England, of the *congé d'élire*. In the[Pg 38] dependency as in England, the State assumed supreme power of religious legislation, overriding and almost treating as null the authority of the ecclesiastical Convocation. Propagation of the Anglican liturgy beyond the Pale continued to be blocked by the language.

Burleigh and the other statesmen of Elizabeth's Council could not fail to turn their minds to the Irish problem, enhanced as its gravity had been by the progress of religious revolution in Europe and the danger of a conflict with the Catholic powers. Trinity College is a noble monument of their policy. In Ireland, as in England, they restored the coin, though the benefits of that wise measure were offset by protectionist enactments carried in the Parliament of the Pale, which bore the usual fruits. They sent commissioners of inquiry to give them more trustworthy information than they could get from the despatches of the deputies or the tattling intriguers of the Pale. They formed a plan for the institution of provincial presidencies to lengthen the arm of government and form local centres of civilization, which, had it taken effect, might have been the best solution of the problem. But the necessary means of giving effect to any policy failed them. Churches and schools, which were named by a[Pg 39] reformer at the time as the indispensable instruments of civilization, could in the case of Ireland be named only in mockery. An ordinance for the general establishment of schools more than once went forth, but an ordinance still it remained. The Pale, reduced as it was in extent and weakly defended, was in itself a nest of misrule, jobbery, and corruption. Nothing could have been done without a military force in the hands of the central government sufficient to enforce law and order. Such a force the counsellors of Elizabeth had no means of maintaining. Continental war drew heavily on the exchequer. The queen was unwisely parsimonious. She was seized with spasms of frugality. Militia on the spot of any value there was none. The service was very unpopular in England, and the men enlisted or pressed for it as soldiers were apt to be of the Falstaffian kind, better at preying on the people for whose protection they were sent and at indulging in the general license of the camp than at facing the perils and hardships of "hostings" in the Irish wilds. Their pay was almost always in arrears.

The service was not inviting. "The deputy, according to his commission, marched into the north. But, alas, he neither found France to travel[Pg 40] in nor Frenchmen to fight withal. There were no glorious towns to load the soldiers home with spoils, nor pleasant vineyards to refresh them with wine. Here were no plentiful markets to supply the salary of the army if they wanted, or stood in need; here were no cities of refuge, nor places of garrison to retire into, in the times of danger and extremity of weather; here were no musters ordered, no lieutenants of shires to raise new armies; here was no supplement of men or provisions, especially of Irish against Irish; nor any one promise kept according to his expectation; here were, in plain terms, bogs and woods to be in, fogs and mists to trouble you, grass and fern to welcome your horses and corrupt and putrefy your bodies; here was killing of kine and eating fresh beef, to breed diseases; here was oats without bread, and fire without food; here were smoky cabins and nasty holes; here were bogs on the tops of mountains, and few passages, but over marshes, or through strange places; here was retiring into fastnesses, glens, and no fighting, but when they pleased themselves; here was ground enough to bury your people in being dead, but no place to please them while alive; here you might spend what you brought with you, but be assured there was no hopes of relief; here was room for[Pg 41] all your losses, but scarce a castle to receive your spoil and treasure. To conclude: here was all glory and virtue buried in obscurity and oblivion, and not so much as a glimmering hope that how valiantly soever a man demeaned himself it should be registered or remembered."

The deputies sent in command might do their best according to their lights. They generally did. But the lights of all of them were not the same, and the web of Penelope woven by one was always in danger of being unwoven by his successor. One of them only, Sussex, was large-minded enough to think of acknowledging the Brehon law, reducing it to a system, and making it a bridge across which the Irish might pass to legal civilization. All the deputies had to contend more or less with local opposition and intrigue.

The consequences to Ireland of this policy of government by deputies were disastrous. The presence of royalty might have had some effect on the Irish heart. It could hardly have failed, at all events, to reveal the real state of things. But it was never tried.

Elizabeth, Protestant by circumstance and profession, Catholic in her real leanings, hating nothing so much as a Puritan, unless it were a [Pg 42]clergyman's wife, and an autocrat to the core, had no desire of breaking with the Papacy or with Spain. But when a Pope excommunicated and deposed her, the die was cast. Ireland was drawn into the European war between Catholicism and Protestantism which was also that between despotism and freedom; she became a point of military danger in a national and religious struggle for life or death. There is now an end of the policy of conciliation or of colonization with a civilizing object. The policy henceforth is that of conquest, and when resistance is obstinate, of extermination.

The reign was filled with successive wars between the English and the natives, the first slightly, the last two more deeply, identified on the side of the natives with papal suzerainty and the Catholic cause. The first was that with Shane O'Neill, elective head of the great Ulster sept of O'Neill and pretender to the royal earldom of Tyrone. The tribal headship was unquestionably elective; to the earldom Shane's claim was doubtful, the question being partly one between the English and the Brehon law. It was presently settled by the murder of Shane's rival. Shane was, in fact admitted himself to be, a barbarian, brutal, drunken, and cruel, all in a high degree. He made his[Pg 43] prisoners wear an iron collar fastened by a short chain to gyves on their ankles so that they could neither stand nor lie. At the same time he was able, crafty, and daring. He made himself supreme in Ulster, baffled the English in war, and was so formidable that the Lord Deputy Sussex, once at least, if not more than once, attempted to get rid of him by assassination. He intrigued with Philip of Spain. At another time he coquetted with the Queen's government and paid a visit to the court, where he and his gallowglasses, with their axes, their Irish heads of hair and moustaches, their wide-sleeved saffron shirts, short tunics, and shaggy cloaks of fur or frieze, produced a sensation among the courtiers. Master of dissimulation, Shane fell on his knees before the Queen and confessed his rebellion in the Irish language "with howling." Returning to Ulster, he recommenced the game there, plundering and burning, slaying man, woman, and child. He was at last stabbed in a brawl with the Scottish raiders with whom he had intrigued. These marauding immigrants from the Scottish Highlands and isles were now a formidable addition to the elements in the cauldron of Irish anarchy and ruin.

Shane was an Irish leader of the thoroughly[Pg 44] Celtic type. Perhaps the next, though in a widely different guise and sphere, may be said to have been Daniel O'Connell.

As a mover of disturbance on a large scale there succeeded James Fitzmaurice, kinsman of the Earl of Desmond, the head of the southern sept of Geraldines. Fitzmaurice, whether from conviction or policy, gave rebellion a more religious character and connected it with Rome and Madrid, which he visited on missions of intrigue. In this work he had a compeer in Stukely, an adventurer of the kind then common, who also intrigued with the Catholic powers. If their aim was an Irish crown on a Catholic head, it came to nothing. But Fitzmaurice brought with him to Ireland a regular proclamation from the Pope, and had made formidable headway in his appeal to the forces of disorder when he was killed. The leadership of the movement passed to the Earl of Desmond, who with a little aid from Spain raised in Munster a rebellion on a large scale. He was a feeble though respectable leader, and his rising in the end bore no fruits but a renewal of slaughter and devastation.

The aid of Rome and Spain promised to the Irish Catholics was long in coming. Ever tardy and vacillating was the mind of the Spanish king. But at[Pg 45] the time of Desmond's rebellion the aid came. In concert with the insurgent Irish a force of Italians and Spaniards landed and established itself in a fortalice at Smerwick. The deputy at that time was Lord Grey, a Puritan most pronounced and militant, the Artegal, the Knight of Justice, in Spenser's "Faerie Queene," bent on the overthrow of the false Duessa and the extermination of her brood. He invested Smerwick. The Irish allies of the invader failed to relieve the place, and the garrison was compelled to surrender at discretion. Grey then butchered the whole of them in cold blood. Raleigh, as the officer in command, it is to be feared directed the slaughter. Alva or Parma would have done the same, and Elizabeth in approving incurred no special infamy.

11

The poor Irish in this rebellion showed that fidelity to a chief which was one of their small stock of political virtues. They afterwards showed their love of legend, of melancholy legend especially, by telling that Desmond's ghost, mounted on a phantom steed with silver shoes, rose at night from the water on the bank of which he had been slain, and fancying that in the moaning of the wind they heard the Desmond howl.

The attainder of the Earl of Desmond was [Pg 46]followed by the sweeping confiscation of a vast tract of land to the Crown, on the assumption that as the domain of an earl it had been a fief and the property of its lord; whereas under native law and according to native ideas it was the property of the tribe. Spenser was one of the grantees of the Crown and settlers on the conquered land. He had been the secretary of Lord Grey. The author of the "Faerie Queene" thus encountered the religion of the false Duessa, his hatred of which was not likely to be diminished when he was afterwards by a great outbreak of insurrection ejected from his grant.

Now along the dangerous western coast of Ireland were driven in dire distress a number of great ships of war, with the troops and much of the power and chivalry of a mighty kingdom on board. These were the miserable remnants of the Invincible Armada. About a score of the ships were cast ashore or wrecked. The crews for the most part perished. On one strand of less than five miles in length were counted above eleven hundred corpses cast up by the sea. On two miles of strand in Sligo there lay wrecked timber enough to build five first-rate ships, besides mighty great boats, cables and other cordage, and masts of extraordinary size. Of those who struggled to land, many were killed by the[Pg 47] English, not a few by the native Irish, who stripped and robbed those whom they did not kill, skipping and capering at the sight of such glorious plunder. The Armada had come to liberate the native Irish from the heretical yoke; but love of plunder overcame in their simple souls regard for a political and ecclesiastical alliance, their appreciation of which, perhaps, had never been very clear.

One Spaniard, Cuellar, after being stripped and narrowly escaping with his life, spent some time in an Irish cabin, and has left his notes on native Irish life and character, valuable as those of a neutral.

"The habit of those savages," he says, "is to live like brutes in the mountains, which are very rugged in the part of Ireland where we were lost. They dwell in thatched cabins. The men are well made, with good features, and as active as deer. They eat but one meal, and that late at night, oatcake and butter being their usual food. They drink sour milk because they have nothing else, for they use no water, though they have the best in the world. At feasts it is their custom to eat half-cooked meat without bread or salt. Their dress matches themselves—tight breeches, and short hose jackets of very coarse texture; over all they wear blankets, and their hair comes over their eyes.[Pg 48] They are great walkers and stand much work, and by continually fighting they keep the queen's English soldiers out of their country, which is nothing but bogs for forty miles either way. Their great delight is robbing one another, so that no day passes without fighting, for whenever the people of one hamlet know that those of another possess cattle or other goods, they immediately make a night attack and kill each other. When the English garrisons find out who has lifted the most cattle, they come down on them, and they have but to retire to the mountains with their wives and herds, having no houses or furniture to lose. They sleep on the ground upon rushes full of water and ice. Most of the women are very pretty, but badly got up, for they wear only a shift and a mantle, and a great linen cloth on the head, rolled over the brow. They are great workers and housewives in their way. These people call themselves Christians, and say Mass. They follow the rule of the Roman Church, but most of their churches, monasteries, and hermitages are dismantled by the English soldiers, and by their local partisans, who are as bad as themselves. In short there is no order nor justice in the country, and every one does that which is right in his own eyes."

[Pg 49]"Savages" Cuellar calls the natives; what but savages could they be when not only had all the means of civilization been withheld from them, but they were hunted like beasts of prey? That the women are "great workers and housewives in their way" is a redeeming feature in the picture. The whole land, English and Irish alike, was a wreck. The secretary of a lord deputy reports that the people had no conscience, but committed crimes freely; that they even changed wives among themselves; that bridges were falling down, churches roofless; there were no charities, no schools; law was jobbery, and the judicial bench was filled with ignorance; every lord hated the restraints of law and made himself an Irish chief; and disorders were as great among English soldiers as among Irish kernes.

The third rebellion, and the most formidable of all, was that of the Earl of Tyrone, head of the O'Neills of Ulster. It stirred the general forces of revolt, national and religious, beyond Ulster, in Connaught and elsewhere. Tyrone gave his movement distinctly the character of a holy war, and received aid from Spain. Unlike Desmond, he was an able leader. He gained a victory over the English at the Yellow Ford which filled Dublin with panic. To put him down, Elizabeth

12

sent her[Pg 50] favourite Essex, with forces greater than her parsimony allowed to an ordinary deputy. Essex went forth with great pomp and amidst high expectations. But he totally lacked steadiness of character and policy. He failed and went home to run mad courses and die on the scaffold, faintly recalling the Irish history of Richard II.

Essex was succeeded by Mountjoy, able, iron-willed, and ruthless, who made it a war of extermination and devastation. The Spaniards brought tardy aid to their Irish allies. They landed in force at Kinsale, and for a moment the fortune of war seemed to waver, but it soon inclined again to the side of the deputy and England. The force of the rebellion was broken, and Tyrone was compelled to surrender.

Of all the wars waged by a half-civilized on a barbarous and despised race, these wars waged by the English on the Irish seem to have been about the most hideous. No quarter was given by the invader to man, woman, or child. The butchering of women and children is repeatedly and brutally avowed. Nothing can be more horrible than the cool satisfaction with which commanders report their massacres. "I was never," said Captain Woodhouse, "so weary with killing of men, for I[Pg 51] protest to God for as fast as I could I did but hough and paunch them." "The number of their fighting men slain and drowned that day," says another commander, "were estimated and numbered to be fourteen hundred or fifteen hundred, besides boys, women, churls, and children, which could not be so few as many more and upwards." Over and over again massacres of people of both sexes and all ages are reported with similar coolness. Another ruffian seems to have put to death children who were held as hostages.

Mountjoy especially used famine deliberately as his instrument of war, and with signal effect. After his work, multitudes lay dead in the ditches of towns and other waste places, with their mouths coloured green by eating docks and nettles. Children were seen eating their mother's corpse. Old women, we are told, lit fires in the woods and ate the children who came to warm themselves. Not only were horses killed and eaten, but cats and dogs, hawks and kites. The wolves, driven by hunger from the woods, killed the enfeebled people. The dead lay unburied or half-buried, the survivors not having strength to dig graves, and dogs ate the remains.

It must be said that the native Irish not only retaliated these cruelties on the English whenever they[Pg 52] could, but committed them on each other. Edward Butler, for example, invades Arra, the district of another clan, harries the country far and wide, breaks open the churches to which the frightened women had fled in the vain hope of sanctuary, and gives the region up for forty-eight hours to plunder and rape, sparing neither age nor condition. The lately gathered corn is destroyed, and famine stares the whole population in the face. The raid is presently repeated, the cattle are driven off, and a house full of women and children is given to the flames. In the English settlement of Munster, overrun by the native Irish, English children are taken from their nurses' breasts and dashed against walls; an Englishman's heart is plucked out in his wife's presence, and she is forced to lend an apron to wipe the murderer's fingers. Of the English fugitives who flocked into Youghal some had lost their tongues and noses. Irish tenants and servants that yesterday fed in the settlers' houses were conspicuous by their cruelty.

What was called law was almost as murderous as war. Men were hanged at assizes by scores, and these massacres were reported by the deputy with satisfaction as gratifying proof of the increased influence of public justice. A bishop witnesses them[Pg 53] with complacency. Respect for human life must have perished. Such was the training which in the formative period of national character the Celtic Irish received, and which must be borne in mind when we come to atrocities committed by them at a not very much later period.

At the same time we do not see the back of destiny's cards. The subjugation of barbarous clans by a foreign conqueror, himself half-civilized, was horrible. Would a series of tribal wars among the clans themselves have been less horrible? When Strongbow landed there had been hardly any sign of permanent union or of the foundation of a settled polity. Nor afterwards does there appear to have been any attempt or tendency of the kind.

Tyrone, on his submission, had been restored to rank and great part of his estate. But he, as well as his confederate, the O'Donnell, created Earl of Tyrconnell, afterwards finding themselves objects of aversion and suspicion, fled the country. Their flight and the suppression of a futile outbreak of tribal insurrection under another O'Donnell finished the work. The whole island was now conquered, but the heart of the people, as presently appeared, was very far from being won. The hold of the Papacy and the Catholic Church upon their liegemen[Pg 54] had been growing stronger under the long struggle and was not impaired by its close. It formed henceforth a religious substitute for nationality.

[Pg 55]

13

V

Ireland, conquered, now became shire land, at least in contemplation of law. The law of England, in the eyes of its professors the consummation of human wisdom, ousted the Brehon law. The feudal system of land tenure supplanted the tribal system. Freehold and leasehold, primogeniture and entail, took the place of tribal ownership and tanistry. Justice was henceforth to be administered in English courts, and judges were to go circuit as in England. The change at first seemed to be well received. Perhaps novelty itself impressed. An English chief justice, going circuit through the newly Anglicized districts, could complacently report that multitudes had flocked to his court; whence he drew the cheerful inference that the Irish after all, like other men, loved justice. So they did, and do; but it was not the justice of the king's bench and Coke. Nor did they love its administration by an alien conqueror. It was probably curiosity as much as confidence that drew them to the court of Chief Justice Davies; so the event proved.

[Pg 56]The whole machinery of government, as well as the law and the judiciary, was at the same time assimilated, formally at least, to the English model. The corporate towns received new charters. The place of the military deputy was taken by the head of a civil government with his officials.

Unhappily the ecclesiastical polity of England, with its tests and its recusancy law, compelling attendance at the services of the State Church, was at the same time thrust upon people to whom it was in itself and in its associations abhorrent. Under Elizabeth there had been a politic laxity. Now fines for recusancy are exacted. Intolerance of Catholic dissent from the royal religion could not fail to be increased by the Gunpowder Plot.

James I., with all his pedantry, his absurdities, and his stuffed breeches, was not without something of the largeness of mind which culture generally imparts. He could understand Bacon. His Irish policy, evidently inspired by Bacon, was colonization, plantation as it then was called. For this there was ample room on the forfeited lands of Tyrone and other attainted chiefs, so far as legal ownership in the contemplation of English law was concerned. But the attainders of the chiefs had not cleared the lands of the members of their septs, in whose minds[Pg 57] tribal ownership was rooted. This was the weak point of the transplantation policy, as in the sequel tragically appeared. Extensive grants, however, were made to a colony formed by English and Scottish settlers, undertakers as they were called. Of Scottish settlers there had before been not a few. The city of London invested largely in the enterprise. Thus was formed in Ulster, and in Ulster has continued to exist to the present time, a sort of Protestant pale. Bacon's philosophic eye ranges complacently over the prospect of a people of barbarous manners "brought to give over and discontinue their customs of revenge and blood and of dissolute life and of theft and rapine, and to give ear to the wisdom of laws and governments; whereupon immediately followeth the cutting of stones for building and habitation, and of trees for the seats of houses, orchards, enclosures, and the like." Beyond doubt this settlement was an improvement in material respects. Nor, though the new settlers might domineer, was their domination likely to be more oppressive and insolent than that of the native chief, with his gallowglasses and his coyne and livery. The tribal ownership of land had probably become almost a fiction, the chief treating the land as his own. Little, therefore, was actually lost in[Pg 58] that way by the tribesman, while there was an end of coyne and livery and the other extortions of the chiefs. On the other hand the chief, however oppressive, was nominally one of the tribe and a kinsman, and the land was still tribal in the fancy of the sept. The tribesman was not liable to eviction. Nor was improvement in agriculture or even in advancement of law and order likely to be so fascinating to the native Irish, especially to gallowglasses and kernes, as to Bacon. The adventurers were apt to be of a sordid class, ravenous, close-fisted, little likely to make themselves beloved. The eagles of enterprise spread their wings for the Spanish main; the vultures swooped upon Ireland. The medley of Brehon law and English law, with the variety of titles, some by forfeiture for treason, others by ancient grants from the Crown, formed an element in which the art of the predatory pettifogger had full play. By legal chicane, the chicane of an alien law, many an Irish Naboth may have been dispossessed. There was, moreover, the antagonism of religion, greatly intensified by the long struggle in which the natives, fighting for independence, had looked up to Rome for support and been fired at heart by the active zeal of her missionaries.

[Pg 59]The government meant well. It sent over an able lord deputy in the person of Chichester, who did his best for healing and improvement. In improvement he was somewhat hasty and procrustean. He might have done better had he only imbibed Bacon's spirit of philosophic toleration, and not fancied that for Irish barbarism Protestantism of the Anglican type was the sovereign cure. Bacon, as one of his three specifics for the recovery of the hearts of the people, had recommended a toleration, partial and temporary at least, of the Catholic religion, which was to be combined "with the sending over of some good preachers, especially of that sort which are vehement and zealous persuaders and not scholastical, to be resident in principal towns." The government issued a politic manifesto, promising to all native Irish of the poorer class equal protection and complete immunity from any oppressive claims of chiefs. But let the government charm as wisely as it might, it could not charm away the difference of race, language, and character, the antagonism of religion, the memories of the long and murderous struggle, the ravenous cupidity and overbearing attitude of the alien adventurer, the anguish of the native who saw the stranger in possession of his land.

[Pg 60]James called a Parliament for all Ireland, Catholic as well as Protestant. It was packed for the Crown, which created boroughs for that purpose. Still, it was something more like a national assembly than Ireland had ever seen or in fact was destined again to see. The elections to it were fiercely contested between the races and religions. Its first sitting was characteristic. There was a division on the election of a speaker. One party went out into the lobby. In its absence the other party seated its man in the chair. The party which had gone out, returning and finding what had been done, seated their man in the other man's lap. The importance of this Parliament, however, is extolled by Sir John Davies, and one act, at all events, stands to its credit. It repealed the statute of Kilkenny and all other laws recognizing and perpetuating distinctions of race, declaring that their cause had ceased, since the inhabitants of the kingdom without distinction were henceforth under the protection of the Crown, and the best way of settling peace was to allow their intercourse and intermarriage so that they might grow into one nation. There was a transient ray of sunlight on the dark scene. Efforts were made to improve Trinity College, and learning shone forth in the person of Usher.

[Pg 61]

VI

There was still in Ireland a mine charged with the wrath of the dispossessed added to the hatred of race and religion, the religious hatred being the more deadly because, the Protestants of Ireland being Calvinist, the antagonism was extreme. The match was applied to the mine by the outbreak of revolution in England under Charles I. Strafford, having passed from the ranks of patriotism to the place left vacant by the death of Buckingham in the councils of the king, came with his dark look of command as viceroy to play the part of beneficent despot in Ireland, and at the same time to raise an army there for his master. The part of despot he played to perfection, making the Irish Parliament the tool of his will, applying to it and to the government in general his own and Laud's high royalist policy of Thorough. The part of beneficent despot he played to a considerable extent. He set his heel on the rapacity of the adventurers, compelling the chief of them, the Earl of Cork, to disgorge. He enforced order and[Pg 62] put down piracy, which in the general disorder had become rife. He fostered the cultivation of flax and the linen trade, though he paid blackmail to English protectionism by prohibiting the woollen manufacture. He did his best to reform the State Church, which he found sunk in torpor, sinecurism, and simony, while its edifices were ruins and piggeries. Unluckily he was a strict Anglican, whereas the only Protestantism in Ireland which had life in it was the Calvinistic Protestantism represented by Usher. He made a mortal enemy by turning the sumptuous monument of Lady Cork off the place of the high altar. But to find means of raising an army for his king he had to resort to violent measures. He dragooned the Parliament into granting extraordinary supplies. The king had pledged himself in the form of "graces" to respect and quiet titles to large tracts of land. These graces Strafford thrust aside. By legal chicane and intimidation of juries he, in defiance of the king's plighted word, confiscated a great part of the land of Connaught. A legal raid of the Crown on the estates which the city of London had purchased in Ulster made the lord deputy another formidable enemy. He added to the number by trampling on the pride of men of rank and influence. Strafford[Pg 63] had formed his army. That he intended it as a support to the arbitrary government of Charles is beyond question; his betrayal of that intention by some loose words uttered in council formed the most damaging piece of evidence against him; and though the army broke up on his departure, fears of it continued to haunt the English mind and to intensify English feeling against the Irish. The Irish Parliament joined in the impeachment of the man who had trampled on it, and when Strafford pleaded in defence of his arbitrary measures, that Ireland was a conquered country, Pym's retort was, "They were a conquered nation! There cannot be a word more pregnant or fruitful in treason than that word is. There are few nations in the world that have not been conquered, and no doubt but the conqueror may give what law he pleases to those that are conquered; but if the succeeding pacts and agreements do not limit and restrain that right, what people can be secure? England hath been conquered, and Wales hath

15

been conquered, and by this reason will be in no better case than Ireland. If the king by the right of a conqueror gives laws to his people, shall not the people by the same reason be restored to the right of the conquered to recover their liberty if they can?"

[Pg 64]Revolution was in the air. It stirred the heart of the Catholic cowering under the penal law, who saw the foot of his arch-enemy the Puritan on the steps of power. It stirred still more the heart of the disinherited native, especially on the forfeited domain of Tyrone. One of those great popular conspiracies of which the Irish have the gift was formed under the leadership of Phelim O'Neill, who ranked among his countrymen as head of the great sept of O'Neill, and cherished ancestral traditions of vast domains and princely power. With Phelim O'Neill was a better man, Roger Moore, one of the disinherited, a deadly enemy of England. The rebellion posed as royalist, declaring for the king against the Puritan and revolutionary Parliament; its aims were Ireland for the Irish, and Catholicism as the Irish religion. Phelim O'Neill was not a man to restrain from crime. But the people, once launched in insurrection, were probably beyond control. They rose upon the English settlers in Ulster, drove them from their homes, and massacred some thousands with the usual cruelty, women and children taking part in the fiendish work. Many were stripped naked and exposed to perish in the cold. Dublin was full of shivering and famished fugitives. The capital[Pg 65] itself narrowly escaped through fortunate betrayal of the plot, such as in an Irish conspiracy seldom fails. It was natural that panic should exaggerate the number murdered, as it was that panic and superstition together should see the spectres of the English who had been drowned by the rebels at Portadown. The effect upon the English, above all upon the Puritan mind, was like that of the Sepoy mutiny and the massacre of Cawnpore. Ruthless retaliation followed. Where the Protestants got the upper hand, Irish men, women, and children were butchered without mercy. Thenceforth the Irishman was to the Puritan a wild beast or worse. All Irishmen who landed in England to fight for the king, with the women who followed their camps, were put to the sword. An Irishwoman left behind by a Munster regiment at the siege of Lyme was torn to pieces by the women of the place.

The English Parliament at once, being short of money, passed, to provide for the Irish war, an act confiscating in advance two and a half millions of acres of rebel land as security for a loan; a measure, to say the least, extreme and sure to make the conflict internecine. The act passed without a dissentient voice, and was one of the last that received the assent of Charles.

[Pg 66]In Ireland against the dark clouds of the storm one rainbow appeared. The Protestant Bishop Bedel, though a proselytizer, had by his beneficence won the love of his Catholic neighbours. He and his family were not only spared by the rebels, but treated with loving-kindness, and when he died a farewell salute was fired over his grave.

Thus commenced a course of mutual slaughter which lasted eleven years, and, according to Sir William Petty, cost, by sword, plague, and famine, the lives of a third part of the population. A great pasture country was reduced to the importation of foreign meat. A traveller could ride twenty or thirty miles without seeing a trace of human life, and wolves, fed on human flesh, multiplied and prowled in packs within a few miles of Dublin. Numbers abandoned the country and enlisted in foreign services. Slave dealers plied their trade and shipped boys and girls to Barbados.

Strafford's place as deputy not having been filled, the government remained in the hands of the Puritan Lords Justices Parsons and Borlase, the first an intriguer and jobber, the second a worn-out soldier and a cipher. They had prorogued the Parliament by which they might have been restrained. The commander of the army on the king's side and the[Pg 67] representative of the king's interest was Ormonde, the head of the loyalist house or sept of Butler, a man thoroughly honourable as well as able and wise, whose character stands out nobly amidst the dark carnival of evil.

It is difficult to say to which of the contending parties the palm of atrocity is to be awarded. Probably to that of the government, which knew no measure in the extermination of Catholics and rebels. Where Ormonde commanded there was sure to have been comparative mercy. Mercy there certainly was on the side of the insurgents when they were commanded by Owen O'Neill, a genuine soldier trained in foreign service and observant of the rules of civilized war. But a papal legate who was in the Catholic camp gleefully reports that after a battle won by the confederates no prisoners had been taken. By the soldiery of the government at least children were butchered, the saying being that "nits make lice."

The anti-Catholic policy of the Puritan government and the castle had driven into the arms of insurrection the Catholic lords of the Pale, English in blood, normally hostile to the tribes though they were. The Confederation formed at Kilkenny a provisional government with an assembly of priests[Pg 68] and laity combined, which elected a council of war. The assembly was presently joined by a papal nuncio, Rinuccini, who brought money from Rome and it seems at the same time encouragement of the rebellion from Richelieu. The nuncio sought to control

16

everything in the paramount interest of the Papacy, which thus once more appears as a power of temporal ambition. The assembly was not unanimous. Of the clergy and the nuncio the chief aims were the ascendency of the Catholic Church and the recovery of the confiscated Church lands. The chief aims of the lay lords were lay; they wanted relief from political disabilities and recovery of their political power. Restoration to the Church of the abbey lands, of the grantees of which they were the heirs, was by no means to their mind.

Of the origin of the rebellion in Ulster King Charles was perfectly innocent, though he drew suspicion on himself by some careless words. Nothing worse for his cause could have happened. But when in his wrestle with the Puritan he was thrown, he began to cast a longing eye on the forces in Ireland which, though rebel and Catholic, were at all events hostile to the Puritan. There ensued a series of tangled intrigues with the Confederates, in the course of which Charles showed his usual[Pg 69] weakness and duplicity, while he was fatally committed by the mingled rashness and tergiversation of his envoy, Glamorgan, the result being a disclosure very injurious to the poor king's character and cause. The Confederacy was divided between a party which was for treating and a party which was for war to the knife. For war to the knife was the nuncio, an ecclesiastical termagant of the Becket stamp, inflated with notions of his own spiritual power and reckless in the pursuit of his own end, which was to lay Ireland at the feet of the Pope. In all this the high-minded Ormonde sadly stooped to take a part for his royal master's sake. When the cause of his royal master was finally lost, he surrendered his command to the Parliament and left Ireland.

After the execution of Charles the scene shifted again. Abhorrence of regicide brought about a junction of the more moderate Protestants with the more moderate Confederates, uniting different parties and sections under a common profession of loyalty. Ormonde then returned to lead a mixed and not very harmonious force against Michael Jones, the Republican commander. He advanced to the attack of Dublin, but was totally defeated by Jones.

[Pg 70]Now on the wings of victory came Cromwell with ten thousand of the New Model. His proclamation on landing promised to all who would keep the peace, peace and protection for themselves. That proclamation, the first utterance of law and order heard in those parts for ten years, was strictly carried into effect. A soldier was hanged for robbing a native of a fowl. No disorder, rapine, or outrage upon women is laid to the charge of the Puritan army in Ireland. Cromwell sat down before Drogheda, which was held by a large royalist garrison, partly English. The garrison having refused to surrender on summons, he stormed. Two attacks failed; a third, led by himself, took the town. He put the garrison to the sword. That a garrison refusing to surrender on summons and standing a storm might be put to the sword was the rule of war in those days; it was the law, though not the rule, of war even in the days of Wellington. Nevertheless, this was a fell act for a commander who was generally humane in war, and at Worcester risked his life in persuading Royalists to take quarter. Of this Cromwell was himself sensible, and he spoke of it with compunction. "I am persuaded," he said in his despatch to the Parliament, "that this is a righteous judgment of God upon[Pg 71] these barbarous wretches who have imbrued their hands in so much innocent blood; and that it will tend to prevent the effusion of blood for the future; which are the satisfactory grounds to such actions, which otherwise cannot but work remorse and regret." Were remorse and regret ever breathed by Alva, Parma, or Tilly? What did the soldiery of those Catholic commanders do when it stormed a Protestant town? What did the British soldiery, maddened by the recollection of a massacre far less than that of 1641 do, not only to the Sepoy mutineer, but to the insurgent people of Oude? When Rupert stormed Leicester, the town was sacked, and women and children were found among the dead. The Royalist Carte, in his life of Ormonde, commenting on the slaughter of the garrison of Drogheda, says, "This was certainly an execrable policy in that regicide. But it had the effect he proposed. It spread abroad the terror of his name; it cut off the best body of the Irish troops and disheartened the rest to such a degree that it was a greater loss in itself and much more fatal in its consequences than the rout at Rathmines." This is not a defence, nor much of an excuse. But it testifies to a motive other than mere thirst of blood and shows that Cromwell spoke the truth.

[Pg 72]There was cruel slaughter again at the storming of Wexford, but it does not appear that it was ordered by Cromwell. The defences having been carried, the combat was renewed within the town by the townspeople, who, it is stated, had provoked wrath by their piracy and by drowning a number of Protestants in a hulk. The city had been summoned to surrender on fair terms.

Cromwell was at once called away to the war with Scotland. He left the war in Ireland to be finished by Ireton and Ludlow, who gradually extinguished organized resistance, leaving only something between guerilla warfare and brigandage called "Toryism," a name presently transmitted to a great political party in England which bore it as a name of honour, in opposition to that of Whig, on every hypothesis equally humble in its source.

The two races and religions had fought for the land, and the Saxon and Protestant had won. It is surely simple to suggest that the winner ought to have invited the loser to take the prize, especially after such a display of that loser's sentiments and intentions as the massacre of 1641. Had it not been made fearfully clear that the two races and religions could not dwell together in peace? The[Pg 73] victorious Puritan drove the Catholic into Connaught. The Catholic, if he could, would have driven the Puritan into the sea. The original decree of "To Hell or Connaught," the hateful sound of which still rings in Irish ears, seems to have been somewhat mitigated as the wrath of the victor cooled. At all events the sentence extended to landowners only, not to artisans and labourers, who were to remain where they were and to be disciplined and civilized by English masters. A great number of those who had fought on the losing side were sent away to foreign service, ridding Ireland of a manifest danger and forming the first instalment of the grand Irish element in the armies of Catholic Europe. There was also a large deportation to Barbados, including probably families left behind by the military emigration. This was cruel work, the more so as there was terrible suffering in the passage. The whole business was horrible and deplorable. But in passing sentence on the winner we must remember what the loser, had he been the winner, would have done. The shadow of an evil destiny was over all. Deportation was not to slavery for life, but to terminable bondage, one degree less cruel.

To cast all on Cromwell is most unfair. He[Pg 74] had nothing specially to do with Ireland till he came to put an end to the war. He left it forever when he had struck his decisive blow. He could no more have given back the contested land to the Catholics than he could have turned the Shannon to its source. The act under which the land had been forfeited in advance and a loan on it raised had been passed by the unanimous vote of Parliament and had received the assent of the king. The soldiers who held land-scrip for their pay presented their claims. As little would it have been possible for Cromwell, even if he had desired it, to license the celebration of the Mass, which in Puritan eyes was a sign, not only of idolatry, but of allegiance to a foreign power, that power the mortal enemy, not of the Protestant religion only, but of the Protestant State. With liberty of conscience Cromwell declared that he would not interfere. This was something in an age when the rack and the stake of the Inquisition were still at work and when Irish troopers in the service of a Catholic power were butchering the Protestant peasantry of Savoy. If the Nuncio Rinuccini had got the upper hand in Ireland, a retirement of heresy into the sanctuary of conscience would scarcely have saved it from the stake. Cromwell does not [Pg 75]appear to have persecuted in Ireland or to have given the word for persecution.

The Protector united Ireland as well as Scotland to England, thus bringing the factions under the control of a strong government, Ireland's only hope of peace. Union assured her free trade with Great Britain and the dependencies, an inestimable boon, not in the way of material wealth only, but in that of commercial civilization, as its withdrawal afterwards fatally proved. Her shipping was at the same time assured of exemption from the disabilities of the Navigation Laws. The Protector sent her a good governor in the person of his son Henry, who seems to have identified himself with the welfare of her people. He sent her a liberal law reformer in the person of Chief Justice Coke, proposing to himself to treat her as a blank paper, whereon he could write reforms such as professional bigotry debarred him from effecting in England. His mortal enemy Clarendon, after dilating on the iniquities of the settlement, says, "And, which is more wonderful, all this was done and settled within little more than two years to that degree of perfection that there were many buildings raised for beauty as well as use, orderly and regular plantations of trees, and fences and enclosures[Pg 76] raised throughout the kingdom, purchases made by one from the other at very valuable rates, and jointures made upon marriages, and all other conveyances and settlements executed, as in a kingdom at peace within itself, and where no doubt could be made of the validity of titles." If these material improvements were at first limited to the domain and race of the victor, they would in time have spread.

Cromwell's own letter to Sadler on the administration of justice in Ireland breathes anything but the ferocity ascribed to him. About religion he speaks in his unctuous Puritan way, but in a tone far from savage. "First let me tell you, in divers places where we come, we find the people very greedy after the Word, and flocking to Christian meetings; much of that prejudice that lies upon poor people in England being a stranger to their minds. And truly we have hoped much of it is done in simplicity; and I mind you the rather of this because it is a sweet symptom, if not an earnest of the good we expect."[1]

His words on the social question in the same letter show tenderness of feeling. "Sir, it seems to me we we have a great opportunity to set up until[Pg 77] the Parliament shall otherwise determine, a way of doing justice among these poor people, which for the uprightness and cheapness of it may exceedingly gain upon them who have been accustomed to as much injustice, tyranny, and oppression from their landlords the great men, and those that should have done them right as (I believe) any people in that which we call Christendom.... Sir, if justice were freely and impartially administered here, the foregoing darkness and corruption would make it look so much the more glorious and beautiful and draw more hearts after it." This is not the language of hatred, much less of extermination.

Critics of Cromwell fail to notice that his mind opened as he rose, notably in the way of religious toleration. The Ironside had now become a great statesman. "Savage" the writer of his domestic letters surely can never have been.

The representatives of Ireland in the Parliament of the Protectorate, it is true, were nominees. A popular election on the morrow of the Civil War, and with its embers still glowing, would have been out of the question. The union of the Parliaments effected, and representation granted, popular election would have come in time. Meantime, there[Pg 78] was the sheltering and controlling authority of the Protector and the Council of State.

To charge Cromwell with having misunderstood the genius of the Irish nation and wronged it by his policy seems absurd. There was, in reality, no Irish nation. There was an island inhabited partly by the wreck of Celtic tribes, partly by conquerors and colonists of another race, the two races differing widely in character, speaking different languages, having antagonistic religions, not alien only, but desperately hostile to each other. Deadly experience had shown that, left to themselves, they could not live at peace. There was no political union, no attachment to a native dynasty, no tradition or sentiment truly national among the wreckage of the septs. The religious bond, it is true, had been greatly strengthened among them by the conflict, and formed something like a national tie. But adaptation of his policy to Catholic character and sentiment could hardly be expected of a Puritan chief in the age of the Spanish Inquisition.

The European war between Catholicism and Protestantism, and the consequent mingling of religious with political strife, were everywhere a fatal stumbling-block to statesmanship in that day. It does not seem that Cromwell dealt with the difficulty[Pg 79] in England or Ireland less wisely and liberally than did statesmanship elsewhere. Perhaps the greater share of liberality was his. The signs of his personal inclination were certainly on the liberal side.

[Pg 80]

VII

The death of the Protector before his hour, and the military anarchy which ensued, brought on the Restoration. The Restoration brought claims on the part of dispossessed Royalism for restitution in both countries. The occupants of confiscated lands in Ireland, seeing what must come, had under the leadership of opportunist politicians, such as Broghill and Cork, worshipped with politic rapture the return of the Royal Sun. The disinherited on the other hand clamorously pressed their claim to restitution. To that claim honour bade and sympathy inclined Charles II. to give ear. But the adventurers were a formidable body, and while their professions were fervently loyal their hands were on their swords. Nor did Protestant England, even in its hot fit of loyalty, love the Irish Catholic or forget the massacre of 1641. There ensued a vast controversy, desperately embarrassing to Clarendon, Charles's chief adviser, to Charles himself no doubt an insufferable bore. Intrigue and[Pg 81] corruption, in which the possessors were strong, contended with argument in the fray. The government at last took refuge in the appointment of a commission instructed to decide claims to restitution on the principle of complicity or non-complicity in the rebellion of 1641; a criterion rather difficult of application, since Charles I. had on the one hand assented to the Act of Forfeiture, and on the other hand by treating with the Confederates had practically recognized their loyalty to the crown. The upshot was an Act of Settlement with a supplementary Act of Explanation, under which the possessors retained about two-thirds of the lands, the disinherited getting the other one-third, eked out with scraps, which by escheat or forfeiture for regicide were at the disposal of the crown. The Act of Settlement was thenceforth in the eyes of the Protestant possessor the great charter of proprietary right, to be upheld at whatever cost; in the eyes of the dispossessed Catholic, the hateful muniment of proprietary wrong, to be cancelled whenever he had the power. The net result of the Act of Settlement and Explanation was that Ulster was left, as it remains, a Protestant pale.

The Anglican State Church recovered all its[Pg 82] possessions and privileges, and was once more planted on the neck of a Catholic people. It is sad to learn that Jeremy Taylor, who, when under persecution, had eloquently defended liberty of prophesying, as a bishop of the restored Irish establishment defended that liberty no more. But how could a hierarch of the State Church of Ireland fail to don its spirit with his mitre?

The whole of the Protector's work was undone. The union of Scotland and Ireland with England was broken. Ireland was again reduced to the state of a dependency, and of a dependency unloved and unrespected, whose interests were to be always sacrificed to those of the country which was the seat of power. Of this she was soon made fatally sensible. Protectionism was the creed of that dark age. Ireland as a fine grazing country had been doing a profitable export trade with England in cattle, pork, bacon, and dairy produce. The English grazier demanded of his Parliament protection against the free importation of food, denounced by him as a "nuisance." On his demand an act was passed prohibiting the trade. Good sense and the public interest struggled hard. The debate was unusually fierce. Ominous expressions of contempt for the Irish were heard,[Pg 83] and led to a challenge. The king had the good sense to disapprove the measure, but gave way, as he was sure to do. The patriotic policy of the grazier triumphed. Irish fish narrowly escaped prohibition at the same time. This was the first of a line of prohibitive acts fatal to the commerce of Ireland and to her commercial civilization. At the same time she came under the Navigation Laws, which were fatal to her shipping trade.

Ireland, however, had the good fortune to be during the greater part of the reign of Charles II. under the government of that Duke of Ormonde who had commanded for the king in the Civil War. The duke was a statesman, like Clarendon and Southampton, of the old and honourable cavalier school, untainted by the political profligacy or the social dissoluteness of the men of the Cabal. He governed as impartially as the anti-Catholic laws and his own strict Anglicanism would let him; did his best to keep the peace between the factions, political and religious; promoted manufactures and trade, encouraged and endowed education, founded a college of medicine, organized a national militia. He heartily identified himself with Irish interests, and opposed the Cattle Act with an energy and a force of argument which entitle his memory[Pg 84] to the respect of free traders. It is the sad truth that of Irish history between the Conquest and the Union the one bright period is the viceroyalty of Ormonde.

Ireland unhappily, though her interests were out of the pale of English care, was not out of the pale of English faction and revolution. The Stuart brothers, plotting with their French patron the subversion of English religion and liberty, looked to Catholic Ireland for help in their plot. They cultivated the Catholic interest there, and against the law promoted Catholics to office and command. Richard Talbot, lying Dick, afterwards Duke of Tyrconnel, one of the lowest of their wonderfully low agents, as well as about the most violent, appeared upon the scene. It was probably by thwarting or refusing to promote this conspiracy that Ormonde, a strict Protestant though of the Anglican school, and constitutional though a monarchist, incurred temporary dismissal from his viceroyalty. Possibly in the same quarter may be sought the explanation of the mysterious attempt at murdering him by Blood, of the criminal connection of the court with whom there can be little doubt. On the other hand, the cruel anti-Catholic panic, created in England by the well-founded suspicion of danger to[Pg 85] Protestantism from Stuart intrigue with France which gave birth to the Popish plot, extended its rage to Ireland. The last and most pitiable of the innocent victims of that frenzy was the Catholic Archbishop Plunket.

[Pg 86]

VIII

Signs of preparation for the Stuart attack on Protestantism and liberty were visible in Ireland as well as in England in the last years of Charles II. But the blow was suspended during the life of the Merry Monarch, who preferred the calm of the seraglio to the stir of a great enterprise, and did not want to go again upon his travels. With the accession of Charles's fanatical and blundering brother, the crisis came. The Viceroy Clarendon, a Tory of Tories, but an Anglican, was deposed from the viceroyalty, and quitted Ireland with a stream of Protestant refugees in his train. Into his place vaulted Dick Talbot, now Duke of Tyrconnel, drunk with the fury of Romanizing and despotic reaction. A Catholic reign of terror set in. Protestants were disarmed; driven from places of authority, political, judicial, or municipal; practically outlawed, plundered, outraged, compelled to fly for their lives. The country seethed with a general orgie of insurrection and revenge. The people swarmed to the standard of Catholic and[Pg 87] agrarian revolution, rather than to that of the English king, for whom they cared little and who cared little for them. Presently came James, ejected from England, with the power of his French patron at his back. Under him a packed Parliament repealed the Act of Settlement by which the Protestants held their lands, proclaiming reconfiscation and expulsion on a vast scale. Not satisfied with this, the Parliament passed a monstrous Act of Attainder against a large portion of the Protestant proprietary. Nor can it be assumed that the frantic hatred which inspired this act would have confined itself to spoliation, for which the repeal of the Act of Settlement might have pretty well sufficed. A long lifetime had not yet passed since 1641. James, who was not an Irish patriot but an English king out of possession, would have vetoed the Act of Attainder had he dared. But he dared not. He even suffered himself in this case to be divested of the royal prerogative of pardon. Another prerogative, that of regulating the coin, he exercised by sanctioning a base issue on a large scale, which, being made legal tender, completed the ruin of the Protestant trader.

But Protestantism, the stern Protestantism of the Calvinist, rallied on its own ground, and behind[Pg 88] the mouldering walls of Derry made against a Catholic host one of the heroic defences of history, a worthy theme in an after time for the most brilliant of historians. In the battle of Newtown Butler, Protestantism again triumphed over odds. Succour at length came from England. It came first in the person of the renowned Schomberg, whose army, however, made up of raw recruits, ill supplied by fraudulent contractors, and filled with disease by the moisture of the climate, miserably rotted. At last the bonfires of jubilant Protestantism announced that William of Orange had landed. On the Boyne he gained a small battle but a great victory, which decided that the Protestant Saxon, not the Catholic Celt, should be master of Ireland. James fled to the luxurious asylum of his French master, and with him fled the last hope of the Catholic cause.

Once more, however, at Aghrim, the Catholic, under the command of the French General St. Ruth, accepted the wager of battle in open field. He fought well, and the fortune of the day wavered, when a cannon shot took off St. Ruth's head. Protestantism owed its victory largely to a regiment of French Huguenots exiled by the bigoted tyranny of their own king.

[Pg 89]All was over in the field. The irresistible Marlborough reduced Cork and Kinsale. But in Limerick, by soldiers pronounced untenable, Catholicism had its Derry. Its hero Sarsfield, by a daring march, cut off William's siege artillery, and, after a fierce assault, gallantly repulsed, William was fain to raise the siege. After his departure Ginkell again invested the place, and Sarsfield, finding that the last hour of the last Catholic stronghold had come, capitulated on terms. The military terms of the surrender were strictly observed. The political terms, securing a measure of religious liberty to Catholics, though endorsed by William in his wise Dutch love of toleration, were repudiated by Parliament. The "violated treaty of Limerick" was an ugly business, though there seems to have been no protest at the time. But James had fled. The garrison of Limerick had no status but a military one, to which surrender put an end. Politically they were merely insurgents. Could any political terms made with them have bound the sovereign authority of the Irish and British Parliaments in dealing with their own citizens forever? Can Sarsfield have thought that they did?

A crowd of Irish women and children lined the shore at Limerick, watching with tearful eyes the[Pg 90] receding sails of the fleet which bore away their husbands and fathers, the garrison of the last Catholic stronghold, to service in foreign lands. The defenders of Limerick were thus exchanged for the Huguenot exiles who had charged and conquered at Aghrim. Those men, with many an exile from Catholic Ireland who followed in their track, went to form the Irish brigade and to redeem on foreign fields battles lost in their own land.

[Pg 91]

IX

In that mortal struggle, had the Catholic won, he would have deprived the Protestant certainly of his land, perhaps of his life. The Protestant, having won, proceeded at once to avenge and secure himself by binding down his vanquished foe with chains of iron. Chains of iron indeed they were. By the series of enactments called the Penal Code, passed by the Irish Parliament with some assistance from that of England, the Irish Catholic was reduced to helotage political and social, while measures were taken for the extirpation of his religion. To crush him politically he was excluded from Parliament, from the franchise, from municipal office, from the magistracy, from the jury box, as well as from public appointments of all kinds, and even from the police force. To crush him socially he was excluded from all the higher callings but that of medicine, from the bench, from the bar, and from the army. He was denied the armorial bearings which denoted a gentleman. To divorce him from the land, he was forbidden to acquire[Pg 92] freehold or a lease beneficial beyond a certain rate; he was debarred from bequeathing his estate; and his estate was broken up by making it heritable in gavelkind. The gate of knowledge was closed against him. He was shut out of the university; forbidden to open a school; forbidden to send his children abroad for education. That he might never rise against oppression, he was disarmed and prohibited from keeping a horse of more than five pounds' value. He might not even be a gamekeeper or a watchman.

The law, without actually prohibiting the Catholic religion, provided, as was hoped, for its extirpation. All priests were required to be registered, and were forbidden to perform service out of their own parish. All Catholic archbishops and bishops were banished, and were made punishable with death if they returned, so that in future there could be no ordinations. Monks and friars also were banished. Catholic chapels might not have bells or steeples. There were to be no pilgrimages or wayside crosses. Rewards were offered to informers against Catholic bishops, priests, and schoolmasters, and their trade was lauded as honourable service to the state. Marriage of a Catholic with a Protestant was prohibited; to perform it was a capital offence; so[Pg 93]was conversion of a Protestant to Catholicism. Religious hatred outraged domestic affection by enacting that if the son of a Catholic turned Protestant the inheritance should at once vest in him, his father being reduced to a life interest; that the wife of a Catholic turning Protestant should be set free from her husband's control and entitled to a settlement; that a Catholic could not be a guardian, so that, dying, he had to leave his children to the guardianship of an enemy of their faith.

Representatives of the government designated the Catholics officially as "our enemies." The Irish Parliament was exhorted to put an end to all distinctions except that between Protestant and Papist. To such a relation between races under the same government history can scarcely show a parallel, unless it be the case of the Moriscos in Spain.

"It was," says Burke, "a complete system full of coherence and consistency; well digested and well composed in all its parts. It was a machine of wise and elaborate contrivance and was as well fitted for the oppression, impoverishment, and degradation of a people and the debasement in them of human nature itself as ever proceeded from the perverted ingenuity of man." It was the panic rage of a garrison which had narrowly escaped[Pg 94] extermination, and less cruel than the treatment of the Huguenots by the Catholic king at the instigation of the Jesuit and with the approbation of the Catholic Church in France. The fires of the Inquisition were still burning, and continued for some time to burn. If the British Parliament shares the guilt of the Penal Code, twice had an army of Irish Catholics been raised for the destruction of English liberties. When last those liberties were in the extremity of peril, a force of Irish Catholics had been encamped at Hounslow. Nor was Catholicism merely a religion. It was allegiance to a power which claimed the suzerainty of Ireland, which had launched the decree of deposition against Elizabeth, which, after the rising of 1641, had sent its nuncio to the rebel council of Kilkenny. These memories on both sides ought long ago to have been consigned to a common grave.

At the same time it was deplorable that the settlement of the Catholic provinces after their reconquest should have been left to the Protestants of Ireland, transported with rage and fear. The true course, had it been possible, was the union of Ireland with England. Representatives of the loyal districts of Ireland might have been called at once to the Parliament at Westminster. The rest of the island[Pg 95] might have been placed under a strong government of pacification and settlement, till peace and the reign of law had been thoroughly restored. It is needless to say that such a solution could not even suggest itself to the mind of any statesman at that time.

In extirpating the Catholic religion the policy of the Penal Code failed. To the faith which was their only comfort and sole redemption from utter degradation the people more than ever clung. The priests braved the law, celebrated mass in hiding-places, furtively ordained, several hands being laid on at once that the man ordained might be able to swear that he did not know who had ordained him. They taught in hedge schools, and, though but coarsely educated themselves, preserved the scantling there was of knowledge and civilization among the people. In their celibacy they had a great advantage for such work. Interested conversions among Catholics of the higher class, especially as passports to the bar, seem not to have been uncommon. An old lady of an ancient line is said to have embraced Protestantism avowedly against her conscience, saying that it was better that one old woman should burn than that the estates of the house of Tomond should go out of the family. But[Pg 96] disinterested conversions there were none. On the other hand Protestants in isolated settlements were turned Catholic by social contagion.

Other parts of the code took deadly effect. The Catholics generally ceased to own land. Of their landed gentry, some went into exile. The people, bereft of their natural leaders, sank into apathetic helotage and mute despair. Neither in 1715 nor in 1745, when a pretender again unfurled the banner of the House of Stuart, was there the slightest political movement among them. Socially, the iron had entered their souls and they cowered under the yoke of the ascendancy. Once, an informer having tendered a Catholic the legal ten pounds for his pair of fine horses, the Catholic drew his pistol and shot the pair. But this was a rare spark of self-respect on the part of the helot.

The cup of woe was not yet full. In England, with revolution principles, the mercantile party had mounted to power, and commerce in those days was everywhere ridden by the fallacy of protectionism, which killed the only good articles in the Treaty of Utrecht, those opening free

22

trade with France. Ireland, the English protectionist regarded as a foreign country, and a particularly dangerous enemy to his interest. The cattle trade[Pg 97] having been killed by the act of Charles II., the Irish had taken to the export trade in wool and to woollen manufactures. The wool grown on Irish sheepwalks was of the finest, and was eagerly purchased by France and Spain. This industry also English monopoly killed by prohibiting the exportation of wool to foreign countries and the importation of Irish woollen goods into England. The same jealous rapacity seems to have successively killed or crippled the cotton industry, the glove-making industry, the glass industry, the brewing industry, to each of which Ireland successively turned; English greed being bent, not only on excluding the Irish competitor from its own market, but on keeping the Irish market to itself. Ireland had been promised free enjoyment of the linen trade, which Strafford had encouraged by promoting the growing of flax while he discouraged the wool trade; yet even this promise Irish financiers could accuse England of eluding by tricks of the tariff. England needing more bar iron than she could produce, the importation of bar iron from Ireland was allowed; but the consequence was a consumption of timber for smelting which denuded Ireland of her forests.

Cromwell's union would have secured to [Pg 98]Ireland exemption from the disabilities of the Navigation Laws. The Restoration imposed them. They killed her trade with the colonies and killed her shipping interest at the same time. "The conveniency of ports and harbours," said Swift, "which nature has bestowed so liberally upon this kingdom, is of no more use to us than a beautiful prospect to a man shut up in a dungeon."

In all this Ireland was treated as a colony, meant only to be a feeder to the imperial country. But her position was worse than that of the colonies, in which commercial restrictions generally were loosely enforced, and which, when strict enforcement was attempted by Grenville, rose in arms. The colonies, moreover, were regarded with pride and affection. Popish Ireland was regarded with contempt and hatred.

The lawful trade in wool with foreign countries England had suppressed. Its place was partly taken by a smuggling trade, for which the inlets of the Irish coast afforded the best of havens, and which had the people everywhere for confederates. Thus, in every line, religious, social, educational, and commercial, the Irishman found the law his inveterate enemy. Could he fail to be an inveterate enemy of the law?

[Pg 99]Cut off from manufactures and from trade, the people were thrown for subsistence wholly on the land, and land for the most part better suited for pasture than for tillage. For the land they competed with the eagerness of despair, undertaking to pay for their little lots rents which left them and their families less than a bare subsistence. On such a scene of misery as the abodes of the Irish cotters the sun has rarely looked down. Their homes were the most miserable hovels, chimneyless, filthy. Of decent clothing they were destitute. Their food was the potato; sometimes they bled their cattle and mixed the blood with sorrel. The old and sick were everywhere dying by cold and hunger, and rotting amidst filth and vermin. When the potato failed, as it often did, came famine, with disease in its train. Want and misery were in every face; the roads were spread with dead and dying; there were sometimes none to bear the dead to the grave and they were buried in the fields and ditches where they perished. Fluxes and malignant fevers followed, laying whole villages waste. "I have seen," says a witness, "the labourer endeavouring to work at his spade, but fainting for want of food, and forced to omit it. I have seen the helpless orphan exposed on[Pg 100] the dunghill, and none to take him in for fear of infection. And I have seen the hungry infant sucking at the breast of the already expired parent."[2]There was an enormous amount of vagrancy and mendicity, as there was in Scotland before the union. This was under the government of the first of free nations, and in the era of Newton, Addison, and Pope.

Reduced to living like beasts, the people multiplied their kind with animal recklessness. The result was fatal overpopulation, the pressure of which, aggravated by occasional failures of the treacherous potato, could be relieved only by the tragic remedy of emigration on an immense scale.

Of the landowners, who might have had compassion on their serfs, many were absentees; residence in Ireland, especially when agrarian war began, being hardly pleasant. Their place was taken by the middleman, through whose ruthless agency they extorted their rents and who frequently sublet, sometimes even three or four deep, so that the cotter groaned under a hierarchy of extortion. From the ranks of the middlemen were partly drawn the upstart gentry, or squireens, a roistering, debauched, drinking, and duelling crew, whose[Pg 101] tyrannical insolence scandalized Arthur Young, ruling with the horse-whip a peasantry cowering under the lash and hopeless of redress by the law. The peasantry still largely spoke Erse, another badge of their social inferiority, and a further barrier between them and the ruling class.

To the extortion of the middleman was added that, even more hated, of the tithe proctor. The Protectorate had at all events relieved Ireland of the Anglican State Church. That incubus the monarchy reimposed, and the peasant was compelled out of the miserable produce of his potato field or patch of oats, besides the exorbitant rent, not only to provide for his own priest, but to pay tithe to a clergy whose mission was to extirpate the peasant's religion. The Anglican bishoprics were rich. The rectories for the most part were miserably poor, so that pluralism might be necessary to make an income. But pluralism of the most scandalous kind also prevailed, and we have a dean holding two groups of livings, fourteen livings in all, one group twelve miles away from the other. Some of the clergy, on the plea that there were no glebe houses for them, were drawing their tithes in the pump room and at the card tables of Bath. Bishops were sometimes non-resident as well as[Pg 102] scandalously secular and inert. Most of them were English, and appointed to keep up the English interest. There were bright exceptions, such as Bolter, King, above all Berkeley, but they were few. Swift could say of Irish bishops that government no doubt appointed good men, but they were always murdered on Hounslow Heath by the highwaymen, who took their credentials, personated them, and were installed in their place. There have been worse institutions than the State Church of Ireland; there was never a greater scandal. Even if Anglicanism had been less alien to the Irish heart, what chance would such missionaries as these have had against the devoted emissaries of Rome? What must have been the feelings of the Irish peasant when of his crop of potatoes, all too scanty for him and his children, the tithe proctor came to claim a tenth part in the name of a Christian minister?

There were prelates of a better stamp who sought to do well by the people. Under their auspices were set up the chartered schools, to give poor Irish children an industrial education. But the work of charity was marred by bigotry. The children were taken from their Catholic parents and forcibly brought up as Protestants, whereby the heart of the Catholic parent was filled with[Pg 103] anguish, and more bitter offence, it seems, was given than by any other kind of repression. The schools at last became a sink of abuse, inhumanity, and corruption.

Rural Ireland was a recruiting ground for the armies of the Continent. On some lonely hillside the recruiting agent reviewed the youth of the neighbourhood, picked out the strong, the flower of the population, and turned back the feeble to their miserable homes.

If anything was to be done for the extension of Protestantism, union among the Protestant minority was indispensable, and the enthusiasm of the Calvinist, sombre as it was, might have had its attractions for the Celt, as it had for the Celts of the Scottish Highlands, among whom it gave birth to the hill preachers, and for those of Wales with whom Calvinistic Methodism prevailed. But the bishops of the State Church hated the Presbyterian even more bitterly than they hated the Catholic. After their brief and hollow alliance with the Nonconformists, when their own interest was threatened, they had speedily relapsed into High Anglicanism, and under the not unsuitable leadership of the infidel Bolingbroke had taken to persecuting Nonconformity in England. They extended the [Pg 104]persecution to Ireland, excluding by the Sacramental Test the defenders of Derry from municipal office and military service. They imported the Schism Act, forbidding Nonconformists to open schools. They threatened interference with Presbyterian worship, Ireland having no Toleration Act. They disputed the validity of Presbyterian marriage. They thus set flowing a stream of Presbyterian emigration from the north of Ireland to the American colonies. The stream was afterwards swelled by the rapacity of Lord Donegal and other landed proprietors of Ulster, who, being owners of great estates, when the leases of their tenants ran out, instead of renewing them to the tenant, put them up to the highest bidder. Starving Catholics, in the desperate competition for land, outbidding the Protestants, a number of Protestant families were driven from their homes. The consequence was, first, aggressive insurrection under the names of the Heart of Oak Boys and the Steel Boys, ultimately emigration to America. Thus the Church and the landlord between them were charging the mine of American revolution.

[Pg 105]

X

Presently, too, inexorable nature made her voice heard, proclaiming that Ireland, with its rich pastures and watery skies, was in the main not an arable but a grazing country. There was a good market for meat. Speculators began buying up land and throwing it into large grazing farms. The cotter was ejected and driven to the bogs and mountains. This overtaxed even a cotter's submission, and there broke out an agrarian war, the most deadly perhaps in history, the canker and disgrace of British government, protracted in varying phases and with fluctuating intensity almost from that day to this. Companies of men, wearing white shirts over their clothes, and thence afterwards called Whiteboys, harried the grazing farms by night, and the stillness of the night air was broken by the bellowings and moanings of hamstrung cattle.

Irish outrage has been essentially agrarian, rather than religious. The division of churches coincided[Pg 106] generally with the social division. The middleman was necessarily Protestant, since, under the penal law, no Catholic could acquire a beneficial lease; and the antagonism of religion and language emphasized and embittered that of class and interest. But a Catholic generally suffered like a Protestant if he provoked the wrath of the people. A Protestant settling in a Catholic district, if he was in any way obnoxious, was especially liable to maltreatment. Later on there was a hideous instance of this in the case of a Protestant schoolmaster settling and opening his school in a Catholic district. He and his family were mangled with horrible cruelty.

Nor can it be said that the landlords as a class were the objects of hatred and outrage apart from the agrarian quarrel. A landlord who resided and did not oppress his tenantry, especially if he were affable, jovial, and hospitable, was generally the object of a clannish affection, though his mansion might be a "Castle Rack-rent" and his serious duties might be very indifferently performed.

The commercial restrictions and the Navigation Acts were fatal to the prosperity of the whole island, while the penal inability of the Catholics to invest could not fail to lower the value of land.[Pg 107] This would be felt by the conquering as well as by the conquered race and sect. Scotland, cut off by the repeal of Cromwell's union from trade with England and the dependencies, had so suffered commercially and industrially that she swarmed with vagrants, and the ardent patriot, Fletcher of Saltoun, proposed slavery as a remedy for the evil. The union, opening free trade with England, brought commercial prosperity in its train. The English in Ireland stretched out their hands to the British government for a union like that which was being made with Scotland, and were coldly repelled. To English protectionism the chief blame for the refusal no doubt is due. But unwillingness to incorporate a large Catholic population may also have played its part. Let the cause have been what it may, there is hardly anything in the records of British statesmanship more deplorable than this refusal of union to Ireland. Protectionism here again pleads the excuse of universal delusion, and in no case is the excuse more needed.

Moreover, the Protestants of Ireland, British in blood and, as lords over a subject race in their own country, more than British in pride, were denied the enjoyment of British freedom. A Parliament they had; but that Parliament could legislate only[Pg 108] by grace of the English council and of a council named by the lord lieutenant in Ireland. Its control even of money bills was not recognized, while the Crown had a hereditary revenue which made it almost independent of Parliamentary grants. In the Upper House, owing to the large absenteeism of lay lords, the bench of bishops, nominees of the Crown and agents of the British interest, largely held sway. Of the three hundred seats in the House of Commons more than half were filled by nominees of the patrons of pocket boroughs, which the Crown had been always creating at its will, and the nominations were sold like common merchandise. The House, moreover, swarmed with placemen and pensioners. The Parliament was elected for a whole reign, so as to be scarcely responsible even to such a constituency as it had. The Irish Parliament of George II. continued for thirty-three years. There was a session only in every other year. The English House of Lords arrogated to itself the jurisdiction of final appeal. The judges held only during pleasure. There was no annual Mutiny Act. There was no Habeas Corpus. There were large sinecures, instruments of corruption in the hands of the government. The pension list, swollen beyond bounds, was a privy fund for kings' mistresses and[Pg 109] for jobs too dirty for the English list. The high appointments, ecclesiastical, administrative, and judicial, were treated as patronage by the English government and generally reserved for Englishmen. The face of their king the Irish never saw. The viceroy resided only during a small part of his term, and his place was filled in his absence by lords justices who were often bishops, English themselves, and bent above all things on securing the ascendancy of the English interest. Three archbishops in succession practically ruled Ireland. Presbyterians and other Protestant Dissenters, victims of episcopal intolerance, had crying wrongs of their own.

Union with England had been refused, and the protection of England being no longer so manifestly indispensable to her garrison in Ireland as it had been, a craving for self-government took its place. Molyneux, and after him Lucas, alarmed and exasperated authority by writing in favour of the independence of the Irish Parliament. But a far more potent artificer of discord appeared in Swift, who, balked of preferment in England by the wreck of his political party, exiled to a native land which he abhorred, was eating his heart, and ripe for mischief, especially for any mischief which could avenge him[Pg 110] on the Whig government, above all on Walpole, its chief, by whom it seems the path of this model Christian and pure writer to a bishopric had been crossed. That a feeling of justice and of pity for the sufferings of the Irish people, which Swift has vividly described, had their place in his heart beside malice and vengeance, may be true; though his sense of justice was not strong enough to prevent him, profane and really sceptical as he was, from vehemently upholding the Penal Code and the Sacramental Test; while his pity for the people led to no philanthropic effort of a practical kind, and was not very tenderly expressed in his satirical suggestion that they should appease their hunger by eating their babies. His proposal to exclude English goods would gratify his malice as well as his patriotism, and had it been adopted would probably have led to a large increase of smuggling.

One of the grievances of Ireland was that there was no Irish mint. A new copper coinage was needed. The contract was given by the English government to the king's mistress, and by her sold to Wood, a respectable manufacturer. As the coinage was approved by Sir Isaac Newton, then master of the mint, it can hardly have been very bad. But Irish jealousy cast suspicion upon its[Pg 111] character. Then rose a storm of popular fury, improved by Swift into a whirlwind on which he rode in his glory. Swift's "Drapier Letters" are monuments of his genius for pamphleteering, his intense malice, and his freedom from the restraints of truth. They produced an immense effect, made him the idol of Dublin for the rest of his days, and forced Walpole to give way and call in the halfpence. Their author did not mention among the evils of an English connection that he and the members of his State Church were enabled by the support of the British power to set their feet upon the necks of four-fifths of the Irish people and to wring from the starving Catholic the income of the dean of St. Patrick. The letters ranged far beyond the immediate occasion, and appealed strongly to the growing desire of independence, which we may be pretty sure that Swift, had he been nominated by Bolingbroke to an English bishopric, would have fiercely opposed. The Parliament to which his revolution would have consigned Ireland is described by himself as a den of thieves of which he devoutly desired the extirpation.

Presently there arose a patriot party in the Irish Parliament. It found a leader in Flood, a man of solid ability and powerful in debate, while the purity[Pg 112] of his patriotism was not so clear. At Flood's side, or rather perhaps, as the event proved, on his flank, there presently arose the far more illustrious Grattan, whose purity and patriotism were unquestionable, whose oratory was brilliant, his admirers thought divine. The objects sought by the patriots were reduction of the duration of Parliaments, control of money bills, an annual Mutiny Bill, Habeas Corpus, tenure of the judges during life or good behaviour, reduction of the pension list, exclusion of placemen and pensioners from the House of Commons, taxation of the rents of absentees. On the first and most important point they succeeded through a bargain with the Crown on the amount of the military force. The duration of Parliament was cut down to eight years, that number being preferred to seven, because it was only in alternate years that Parliament sat. This was a very important change. War, with imperfect success, was waged on the question of money bills. On the other points reform made no way, the English government clinging obstinately to all its powers and using its veto, while the lord lieutenant was able to avert a crash by buying up a majority in the Irish Parliament. Taxation of the rents of absentees, a measure very popular and much pressed,[Pg 113] was vetoed by the English government. The protest of the absentees against it was evidently the work of Burke, whose patron, Lord Rockingham, had an estate in Ireland. Burke argued that the double land-ownership was a link of union between the two countries; which it might have been if the residence as well as the proprietorship had been shared. The advocates of the tax might have cited the original character of land grants to which feudal service was annexed and which were forfeited by the failure of absentees to perform it. Chatham supported the tax. For a moment, unhappily for a moment only, his thoughts were turned to Ireland. A far greater service he would have rendered his country by pacifying Ireland as he pacified the Highlands than by his conquest of Canada, of which the loss of the American colonies was the result. In the background there was a growing sentiment in favour of independence, the flag of which was by Grattan presently unfurled.

It was not in Ireland as it was in England, where the regular party system prevailed and the minority changed with the majority in Parliament. The Castle called to the council whom it pleased, without regard to the existence of a political connection among them, though it was, of course, under the[Pg 114] necessity of calling those who could bring it support at the time. The party tie was accordingly very loose and connections were shifting. Flood had no scruple in providing for himself, apart from his friends, by acceptance of a rich sinecure under the government. Hely Hutchinson, a free lance, could use his personal influence in forcing the government to make him provost of Trinity College.

For a time the Castle put itself into the hands of a junto of great lords and owners of Parliamentary boroughs, who undertook to supply it with a majority at the price of patronage and power. To break this ring and restore the free action of government, an effort was made by the Lord Lieutenant Townshend. But Townshend's boisterous energy, successful for a time, in the end failed, and the Castle fell back into the routine of government by intrigue and corruption, aided by viceregal dinners and balls.

Chatham's glory dazzled Ireland as well as England. But presently came the quarrel ending in war, with the American colonies, whose commercial grievances were the same in kind as those of Ireland, practically less severe. Ireland at once showed sympathy with American revolt. Presently the island was divested of troops by the demands of[Pg 115] the war, and its coasts were left open to the attacks of privateers. There was no national militia. Under the leadership of Lord Charlemont a body of volunteers, almost entirely Protestant, was raised and reached at last the number of forty thousand. There was, no doubt, in the movement a good deal of claret and fanfaronade. But it included the leading gentry, and for its purpose was very strong. Formed ostensibly, at first really, for defence against the Americans, it presently fell politically into their track and demanded of the British government, now prostrated by misfortune in the war and by the combination of European powers against it, first freedom from the commercial restrictions, then legislative independence. North made commercial concessions; he would have made them on a much more liberal scale and possibly have satisfied the volunteers. But again monopolist greed, strong in the commercial cities of England, vetoed, and Burke lost his seat at Bristol for advocating the policy of free trade. The victories of Rodney and Eliot, had they come in time, might have strengthened the hands of the British government and saved it from an ignominious capitulation. As it was, the British government surrendered at discretion. First the commercial restrictions were swept away; then the[Pg 116] legislative supremacy of England, embodied in the Poynings Act and the Act of the Sixth of George I., affirming the right of the British Parliament to legislate for Ireland, was renounced. Flood, the patriot with a bend sinister, insisted on pushing the humiliation of England still further and compelling her by a declaratory act solemnly to bind her own hands for the future, while Grattan, the patriot without reproach, took the more generous line. Thus England underwent the deepest humiliation in her history at the hands of an Irish party which owed its land, its ascendancy, probably its very existence, to her protecting power. Such was the condign punishment of a long course of ignorant, blundering, and corrupt misgovernment, a punishment not the less calamitous and degrading because it was deserved.

So Grattan in the Irish Parliament was able, in a transport of rhetorical rapture, to worship "the newborn nation," a nation which comprised a fraction of the people of the country, the rest being still political helots. Had he adored an uncontrolled Ascendancy, his deity would have been real.

The volunteers, having felt their strength, were inclined to vote themselves permanent, overawe Parliament, and enforce Parliamentary reform.[Pg 117] Flood was so misguided as to take that line. But the incarnation of violent counsels was the bishop of Derry, an English nobleman holding an Irish bishopric, a most absurd figure, and probably half insane. His Right Reverence avowed that he looked forward to blood. He paraded before the door of Parliament in a coach and six, dressed in purple with long white gloves and gold tassels depending from them, and with a guard of horse, looking as if he meant to be king. But the Parliament was firm, and Lord Charlemont and other sane leaders were able to control the body, which was drawn, not from a Faubourg St. Antoine, but from the property-owning class under aristocratic leading. Still revolutionary excitement did not die.

What was now the state of things? There were two independent Parliaments, each with full powers of legislation, under the same Crown; that Crown not being invested with authority to control and harmonize the action of the two Parliaments, but being a Crown upon a cushion or little more. The commercial and even the international relations of the two Parliaments might point different ways. There might be a divergence on a question of peace or war; one Parliament declaring for war, the other refusing to vote the supplies. On general questions,[Pg 118] such as commercial and criminal law, opposition was possible to any extent; and considering the feelings towards each other with which the partners set out, was not unlikely to occur. Ireland might even refuse currency to English coin. The monarchical link itself was not quite firm. On the question of the regency, when George III. went mad, the two Parliaments did actually fly apart; the Irish Parliament recognizing, while the British Parliament refused to recognize, the claim of the Prince of Wales to the regency by virtue of his birth. Only the king's recovery averted a collision. Adopted in haste and in a rush of revolutionary ardour, the system was in fact unworkable and must have ended in confusion. Grattan was unquestionably true to British connection. But Grattan was not Ireland, and even he had led in no very loyal attitude the defiance of the British Parliament on the regency question. His statesmanship can hardly have been profound if he fancied that the constitution of 1782 would work.

It is moreover always to be borne in mind that this Parliament was the Parliament of a Protestant ascendancy, representing not one-quarter of the people of Ireland, and that with all its high talk of independence, it still owed, and knew that it owed,[Pg 119] to British protection its

27

power, its privileges, its political pelf, perhaps even the safe possession under the Act of Settlement of lands on which the disinherited still cast a longing and vindictive eye.

How then was the policy of Ireland to be kept from breaking away from that of Great Britain? The practical answer was, by corruption, the means of which at the command of the Castle were, besides office, sinecures, some of them very rich; commands in the army; pensions; bishoprics, with other Church patronage; and peerages. The peerages, though lavishly created, seem to have retained their value. The Parliament, the body on which corruption had to operate, was a Parliament of rotten boroughs, the nominations for which were sold in open market. The House of Commons continued to swarm with placemen and pensioners, whose votes were at the command of government. In the House of Lords the Anglican bishops were strong.

Appended to a report made to Pitt on the political situation in Ireland is the following schedule of corruption:—

"H—— H——, son-in-law to Lord A——, and brought into Parliament by him. Studies the law; wishes to be a commissioner of barracks, or in some similar place. Would go into orders and take a living.

[Pg 120]"H—— D——, brother to Lord C——. Applied for office; but, as no specific promise could be made, has lately voted in opposition. Easy to be had if thought expedient. A silent, gloomy man.

"L—— M——, refuses to accept £500 per annum; states very high pretensions from his skill in House of Commons management; expects £1,000 per annum. N.B.— Be careful of him.

"J—— N——, has been in the army and is now on half pay; wishes a troop of dragoons on full pay. States his pretensions to be fifteen years' service in Parliament. N.B.—Would prefer office to military promotion; but already has, and has long had, a pension. Character, especially on the side of truth, not favourable.

"R—— P——, independent, but well disposed to government. His four sisters have pensions; and his object is a living for his brother.

"T—— P——, brother to Lord L——, and brought in by him. A captain in the navy; wishes for some sinecure employment."

[Pg 121]

XI

There was no lack, say apologists of the Irish Parliament, of useful legislation on subjects with which a landed gentry was qualified to deal. There was a fatal lack of legislation on one momentous subject with which a land-owning gentry ought to be qualified to deal, but from which the Irish Parliament resolutely turned its eyes. For half a century before the union, that body steadfastly abstained from inquiring into the causes of disaffection among the peasantry. It even repressed a report upon the subject which the chairman of the committee had begun to read.

The condition of the peasantry was still horrible and heartrending. The revolution of 1782, by loosening the fetters of trade, had brought increase of prosperity to the merchant and manufacturer. It had brought no relief to the tiller of the soil. A little before this Arthur Young had travelled in Ireland and had been shocked at seeing the insolent despotism of the petty country gentlemen, whom he called the vermin of the kingdom, over their serfs;[Pg 122] the horsewhip freely used, the serf not daring to lift his hand in defence, the total denial of legal redress, since a justice of the peace presuming to issue a summons would at once have been called out. Landlords of consequence had assured Young that many of their cotters would think themselves honoured by having their wives and daughters sent for to the bed of their masters. He had even heard of the lives of people being made free with. The middleman and the tithe-proctor were ruthless as ever. To the payment of tithes a drop of bitterness had been added by the exemption, through an abuse of political influence, of the grazing farms, which left the whole burden of maintaining a hostile Church on the back of the cotter. The peasantry, on the other hand, maddened by suffering, took a fearful revenge on the oppressor or his agents. Agrarian murder and outrage prevailed. There were cruelties worse than murder. Middlemen and tithe-proctors were "carded"; that is, lacerated with boards full of nails drawn down their backs, buried up to their necks in pits full of thorns, made to ride on saddles stuck with spikes, their ears and noses cut off. A clergyman was met riding in great agony with his head wrapped up; his ears and cheeks were found nailed to a post. That the[Pg 123] Irish when excited are capable of dark atrocities is a feature of their character which it is useless to disguise. Debility when excited is apt to be most cruel. The trait showed itself plainly in the hamstringing of soldiers and the houghing

28

of cattle, as well as in the torturing of middlemen and tithe-proctors. Law and police were paralyzed. The peasantry were one vast conspiracy bound together by awful pledges, the betrayal of which was death. No evidence could be obtained though there might be plenty of eye-witnesses. Perjury in the common cause was no sin.

It was supposed that the Whiteboys had their meetings in Catholic chapels. But there is no ground for taxing the Catholic Church as a body with any share in the criminal part of the movement. The Catholic clergy of Ireland were then, as they are now, a peasant clergy, sympathizing with their class. They depended on that class for their stipends. Some of them their sympathy might betray into complicity, more or less active, with agrarian crime. More of them might be guilty of failure to exert their religious authority as ministers of the sacraments, the confessional, and death-bed absolution, on the side of law. But their record on the whole appears to have been as clear as, considering[Pg 124] what persecution they had undergone, and that the law was their enemy as well as the enemy of the peasant, it was reasonable to expect.

The mansion of an unpopular landlord became a besieged fortress. Absenteeism of course increased. To a rather later date belongs the story of an agent who, having complained to his absentee landlord that his life had been threatened, received the reply, "Tell the villains that they need not hope to intimidate me by shooting you."

"I am well acquainted," said a statesman not oversensitive to popular wrongs, "with the Province of Munster, and I know that it is impossible for human wretchedness to exceed that of the miserable tenantry of that province. I know that the unhappy tenantry are ground to powder by relentless landlords. I know that far from being able to give the clergy their just dues, they have not food and raiment for themselves; the landlord grasps the whole. Sorry I am to add that, unsatisfied with present extortion, some landlords have been so base as to instigate the insurgents to rob the clergy of their tithes, not in order to alleviate the distresses of the tenantry, but that they might add the clergy's share to the cruel rack-rents already paid. Sir, I fear it will require the utmost ability of Parliament to come to the root of these evils. The poor people of Munster live in a more abject state of poverty than human nature can be supposed able to bear. Their miseries are intolerable; but they do not originate with the clergy; nor can the legislature stand by and see them take the redress into their own hands. Nothing can be done for their benefit while the country remains in a state of anarchy."

[Pg 125]The miseries might not originate with the clergy, but the popular wrath did originate specially with the exactions of the tithe-proctor. Grattan proposed commutation. But then the tithe of pasture agistment, as it was called, could no longer have been evaded. That simple reform was put off for more than a generation, with the most calamitous results.

Dublin was gay, mansions rose, claret flowed, wit sparkled, the dance went round. Nor was there lack of social polish or of culture of the classical kind. On the other hand, there were extravagance, waste, and debt. Wild and spendthrift characters appear among the leaders and mirrors of society. Beauchamp Bagenal, as Sir Jonah Barrington tells us, "had visited every capital of Europe, and had exhibited the native original character of the Irish gentleman at every place he visited. In the splendour of his travelling establishment, he quite eclipsed the petty potentates with whom Germany was garnished. His person was fine, his manners open and generous, his spirit high, and his liberality profuse. During his tour, he had performed a variety of feats which were emblazoned in Ireland, and endeared him to his countrymen. He had fought a prince; jilted a princess; intoxicated the doge of Venice; carried off a duchess from Madrid; scaled[Pg 126] the walls of a convent in Italy; narrowly escaped the Inquisition at Lisbon; concluded his exploits by a celebrated fencing match at Paris; and he returned to Ireland with a sovereign contempt for all continental men and manners, and an inveterate antipathy to all despotic kings and arbitrary governments."

Duelling was the social law. The attorney-general fought a duel; the provost of Trinity College fought a duel. Refusal of a challenge was social death. The viceroy's secretary, when challenged by a disappointed applicant for place, deemed it necessary to go to the field of honour. Robert Fitzgerald was so addicted to duelling that he wore a chain shirt under his vest.

What can have produced such characters? Was it anything in Irish blood or air, or was it the absence of the commercial element with its sobering influence? The story of Robert Fitzgerald, nephew of the bishop of Derry, seems to bespeak a wild domestic despotism exercised by the squires. Fitzgerald is said to have confined his father in a cave with a muzzled bear. He put to death one of his household, for which, however, he was hanged. The matrimonial adventurer from Ireland was also a figure well known in the sister isle.

[Pg 127]Of intellectual fruit there was not much except oratory, pamphlets, and pasquinades. Swift was an Englishman born in Ireland and banished to the place of his birth. Burke's genius as well as his physiognomy was one-half Irish, and his Irish half had its share in that splendid but mischievous outburst, his essay on the French Revolution. His heart turned to

Ireland, and some of his best thought was given to her case. But he hardly belongs to the Irish Pantheon.

Oratory, both Parliamentary and forensic, flourished. Grattan, Flood, Yelverton, Foster, Fitzgibbon (afterwards Lord Clare), Curran, are great names in their different ways. Nor was the oratory all in the style supposed to be Hibernian. Foster's style, for example, was grave and weighty. So generally was that of Flood.

In Parliament there were lively scenes. Grattan and Flood having parted company in politics, and Flood having defamed Grattan, Grattan poured upon Flood a furious torrent of the most personal invective; telling him that his talents were not so great as his life was infamous; that he had been silent for years and silent for money; that he might be seen passing the doors like a guilty spirit waiting the moment at which he might hop in and give[Pg 128] his venal vote; that he was a kettledrum, battering himself into popularity to catch the vulgar; that he might be seen hovering over the dome like an ill-omened bird of night, with sepulchral note and broken beak (Flood having a broken nose); and winding up by telling him in the face of the country, before all the world, and to his beard, that he was not an honest man. Flood retorted with equal fury, and a wild scene ensued. It is not difficult to believe in the genius or the patriotism of these orators; but it is difficult to believe in their unimpassioned wisdom.

The Penal Code had ere this lost much of its cruelty. Time, security, and intercourse had softened the feeling of the Protestants against the Catholics, whose passive loyalty had been proved by their inaction when Great Britain was twice invaded by Stuart pretenders. The most odious enactments of the code, those which involved personal degradation and outrage on family affection, had fallen into desuetude or been evaded. Protestant friends would hold land for a Catholic in confidential trust, and ostensibly assume the guardianship of his children, leaving the real guardianship to the kin. The attempts of informers to take advantage of forfeitures were discouraged by the courts.[Pg 129]Protestant fanaticism was dying out everywhere except in rural Ulster, and was giving way among the educated to indifference and even to scepticism. The spirit of Voltaire was abroad. Chesterfield, as viceroy, brought it with him, laughing at religious intolerance, and saying that the only Catholic of whom he was afraid was the reigning beauty of Dublin. The whole system of the Catholic Church, though still nominally subsisting only by connivance, was openly and securely carried on. Conspicuous Mass houses were built. The Catholic hierarchy and priesthood were forming friendly relations with a government which had once designated all Catholics as enemies. Catholics of the upper class educated in France came back from the land of the Encyclopædists tinctured with its liberalism. Catholics were admitted by connivance into Trinity College. A central committee had been formed to guard Catholic interests, which in the penal era would have been treason. After 1782, relief bills were passed. Catholicism was recognized by law. All restrictions upon the maintenance of the hierarchy, freedom of ordination, or additions to the priesthood were abrogated. Catholics were made capable of acquiring property in land, though under the guise of leases for nine hundred and ninety-nine[Pg 130] years. The Gavelling Act, passed to break up their estates, was repealed. It was unfortunately too late to restore the Catholic gentry, which had been decimated by the Penal Law. In 1783 a bill was passed opening to Catholics the profession of the law in all its branches and grades except the rank of king's counsel and the judicial bench, repealing the law against the intermarriage of Catholics with Protestants, that against foreign emigration, that making an Anglican license necessary for schools, and that restricting the number of apprentices permitted in Catholic trade. The laws against the possession of arms and the exclusion from command in the army were left. Otherwise of the Penal Code the political disabilities almost alone remained.

The principal relief bill was introduced by Sir Hercules Langrishe, the friend and correspondent on Irish politics of Burke, who pleaded the cause of the Irish Catholics with all the vehemence of his nature, a measure of sympathy with the religion probably mingling in his heart with love of freedom and justice. Burke had less feeling for the grievances of Protestant Dissenters or of Anglican clergymen liberally inclined, who sought the relaxation of tests. He afterwards sent his son, whose ability he fondly overrated, as his representative to Ireland, in the[Pg 131] affairs of which the aspiring youth meddled, and with farcical results.

The Presbyterians of Belfast had before this been relieved of the Test Act and their other religious bonds and humiliations. But the relief had come too late to turn them into good friends of the Anglican Church or of British connection. Revolutionary and republican sentiment had, with religious scepticism, taken root in Belfast.

The revolution of 1782 had not been democratic. The Volunteers were property holders and their leaders were peers. But the withdrawal of the Volunteers was not followed by political calm. Among the populace of Dublin, especially, excitement continued and showed itself detestably by hamstringing British soldiers. The cry was now for two drastic measures of change: the political emancipation of the Catholics, and a reform of Parliament substituting freedom of election for nomination and clearing the legislature of pensioners and placemen. The two combined evidently meant death to Protestant ascendancy and to oligarchy, both of which naturally shrank from suicide.

The struggle grew fierce, and now not only was the American Revolution fresh in recollection, but the French Revolution, advancing with thunder[Pg 132] tread, was filling the minds of the people everywhere, and especially those of the oppressed and suffering, with vague visions and hopes of change. Even to the hovel of the Irish serf, a vague hope, not of a society regenerated on the principles of Rousseau, but of deliverance from the middleman, from the tithe-proctor, and from the English connection, which he thought was at the bottom of all his sufferings, had begun to make its way.

Of reform, the leader was Grattan. Opposition to reform found a mighty champion in Fitzgibbon, afterwards Lord Clare, a strong man, fearless as he was able, and a very powerful speaker, but violent and overbearing, as well as reactionary to a degree which charms the reactionary historian. Fitzgibbon had a very coarse but rather effective shield-bearer in Dr. Duigenan, the son of a Catholic farmer intended for the priesthood, but captured by the Protestant clergyman of his parish.

Grattan and the reform party failed to get admission for Catholics to Parliament. They failed to purify the House itself by substituting free election for nomination boroughs, or by the effective exclusion of pensioners and placemen from the House. They succeeded in extending the electoral franchise to all holders, whether Catholic or Protestant, of[Pg 133] forty-shilling freeholds. Unfortunately, they could hardly have done worse than by giving political power to the mass without its natural leaders. Protestant demagogues playing for the Catholic vote were certain to appear. Another bad effect of the measure was the multiplication of cotter holdings by land-owners who would absolutely control the cotter's vote. On the other hand, to ask the Protestant oligarchy to part with its exclusive possession of Parliament was to ask it, not only to resign power, but even to cast a shadow on its property, for the Act of Settlement had hardly even yet become perfectly sacred as the title-deed of proprietary right. Not all the advocates of Parliamentary reform were in favour of Catholic emancipation. Flood among others was opposed to it.

Of the British government Pitt was now absolute master. Early in his reign he had glanced at Irish politics and it seems had thought of union. But the Channel was still wide and Irish government was still left to the Castle. Pitt, however, had tendered Ireland a commercial agreement framed, like his commercial treaty with France, in the spirit of the first statesman who read Adam Smith. Introduced by him with great ability and at first with general acceptance, his measure in the[Pg 134] end was wrecked by a combination of British protectionism, Whig faction, and Irish jealousy on the subject of legislative independence; to the last of which Fox, carried away by faction, scrupled not to appeal. Commercial union would have strengthened the political connection, and by furthering commercial prosperity might have done something to allay Irish discontent. Latterly, Pitt's thoughts had been engrossed by the struggle with France. They were now turned perforce to the political state of Ireland, which was evidently becoming very perilous; at that time, unfortunately, with no happy result.

The Whigs opposed to the French Revolution, Portland, Spencer, Fitzwilliam, and Windham, had coalesced with Pitt without renouncing their general principles, which they wished to apply to Ireland, regarding that field, it seems, as especially their own. At their instance Fitzwilliam was sent over as viceroy, believing, and it seems with reason, that he bore Catholic emancipation and general reform in his hand; though he had no written instructions, nor, it appears, any verbal instructions sufficiently clear. He went hastily to work, opened his budget of concessions prematurely, and too promptly brandished the besom of administrative reform,[Pg 135]dismissing from office one of the great place-hunting house of Beresford, which by assiduous intrigue had filled the public service with its nominees. The Beresford carried his plaint to the headquarters of the Tory party in London, and told Pitt that Fitzwilliam was turning out all the faithful supporters of the government. What followed is still a mystery. There was a long, unaccountable, and apparently inexcusable silence on the part of Portland, broken at last by disclaimer, rebuke, and recall. Fitzwilliam, stung to fury at this treatment, trampled on official rules and did serious mischief by his publication of confidential letters betraying an incipient design of union, which to Irish patriotism at that time was maddening. At the bottom of all the misunderstanding and trouble was the king, into whose miserable mind had been instilled, it appears by Fitzgibbon, the belief that by consenting to Catholic emancipation he would break his coronation oath. The two great Tory lawyers, Eldon and Kenyon, to their honour, told the king the truth. It seems probable, however, that the union of the coalition government was imperfect, as that of coalition governments is apt to be, and that this may be the account both of the want of clearness in Fitzwilliam's original[Pg 136] instructions and of the strange silence, ending at last in an abrupt dismissal, which ensued.

Fitzwilliam left Dublin amidst passionate demonstrations of popular disappointment and grief. His place was taken by Lord Camden, one of the Tory section of the Pitt government, who came to face Irish rebellion aided by Revolutionary France, while England, placed in extreme peril by French victories and the secession of her allies, was struggling for her life and was unable to afford military support to the government of Ireland.

Catholic emancipation and reform of Parliament, had Fitzwilliam been allowed to grant them, would, Grattan thought, have averted the crisis. They might have staved it off, but it would probably have come in another form. That the new power thus called into being would be as loyal as Grattan himself to British connection was a highly precarious assumption. The course of the French Revolution would have not been stayed, nor would the wild hopes which it excited have been extinguished. The aspirations of Tom Paine's disciples at Belfast would not have ceased. The cotter's hunger would not have been appeased nor would he have been reconciled to the payment of tithe and Church cess. The blind hatred of British connection as the [Pg 137]supposed source of all evil to Ireland would have continued to work. The State Church would at once have been attacked. The Castle government, bereft of its two supports, nomination boroughs and patronage, would inevitably have lost its hold. Chaos would then have come. Material order might have been preserved by a sufficient military force. Otherwise there was apparently nothing for it but union.

In Presbyterian Belfast, hatred of the State Church and the English government which supported it, bred by Episcopal intolerance, had developed, especially among the young men, into rationalism and acceptance of the doctrines, both religious and political, of Tom Paine. The connection of sympathy with the exiles in America had been kept up, and the spirit of the American was combined with that of the French Revolution. Thus was formed the circle of United Irishmen. The professed aim of this association, perhaps originally its real aim, was only the reform of Parliament. But it soon became revolutionary, aiming at independence of England and the foundation of an Irish republic, to be brought about by the aid of revolutionary France. Its soul was Wolfe Tone, a young man of talent, literary and practical, and of generous instincts, wild, dissipated, recklessly adventurous, burning with[Pg 138] hatred of England. Other leading members of the circle were Jackson and Emmett. Most of the set were plebeian. But there was one recruit from the aristocracy, Lord Edward Fitzgerald, son of the Duke of Leinster, fired, like Lafayette, with the enthusiasm of liberty, but distinguished and made an object of sentimental interest only by his rank and by his tragical end.

The outbreak was now imminent. Grattan, with his few steadfast adherents, seceded from Parliament, where he had better have stayed to moderate as far as he could the fury of repression. This he owed to the country on which he had imposed the constitution of 1782, a system fraught, as he might have seen, with disruption and capable of being worked only as it had been worked, by Castle influence. The bond of loyalty to England, which was strong in his own breast, he assumed to be general. Neither he nor, with reverence be it said, Burke, excellent as the general principles of both might be, correctly read the situation, which was one of a very special kind. Burke's letter to Sir Hercules Langrishe on the subject of religious emancipation is accounted one of the greatest of his works. But Fitzgibbon might with reason have replied to it that of the real Irish problem it offered[Pg 139] no practical solution. It did not show how a national Parliament of Ireland, with a great Catholic majority, and uncontrolled by Castle patronage and influence, to which reform would have put an end, could be kept in secure harmony with the Parliament of Great Britain. Burke, however, now and then, glances timidly at the policy of union. Grattan could think of nothing but his two Parliaments linked by eternal affection. After Grattan's secession, the oligarchy closed its ranks, and the Parliament thenceforth went thoroughly with the government, or even beyond it, in the policy of repression.

The Castle understood its danger. In Irish conspiracies the informer is never lacking. Besides, there were Catholics, who though patriots, wishing to avert civil war, communicated with the government, and furnished it with information for that purpose. Among these may fairly be numbered Arthur O'Leary, on whose connection with the government and acceptance of a small pension from it, lately revealed, prejudice pounces as a proof that the best reputed and most eminent of Irish Liberals was a rogue. Arthur O'Leary wrote well, and the spirit of his writings was thoroughly liberal as well as loyal. Nothing seems to have been[Pg 140]expected of him beyond general information of Catholic tendencies and movements such as one who desired to avert civil war might honestly give. By its secret intelligence the government was enabled at a critical moment to seize some of the leaders of the conspiracy, while Lord Edward Fitzgerald met his death in resisting arrest.

The fire, smouldering everywhere, burst into a flame in Armagh, a Protestant district into which Catholics had intruded by outbidding Protestant holders of farms whose leases had expired. The Protestants, banding together under the name of Peep o'Day Boys, proceeded to oust the intruders, burning some of their houses. The Catholics combined for mutual protection under the name of Defenders. Outrages were committed on both sides. In a pitched battle, on a small scale, called the battle of the Diamond, the Catholics were worsted and a number of them were killed. Many Catholics were driven from their homes, and the fugitives spread through the country the belief that the Protestants were bent on extermination.

The United Irishmen, disciples of Tom Paine, cared nothing for the quarrels of sects. But disaffection of any kind was grist to their revolutionary mill. They coalesced with Defenderism, and by[Pg 141]superior intelligence got control of the movement, which they organized as an expectant army of revolution. Their task was made easy by the habits of conspiracy formed among the peasantry in the agrarian war. There were secret oaths, passwords, military gradations of command. There were even reviews under pretence of digging the potatoes of patriots who were in prison. Everything was ready for a rising as soon as French succour should appear. All the blacksmiths were making pike-heads, the young trees were being everywhere cut down for the shafts. Muskets in plenty would come with the auxiliary army from France. Wolfe Tone had visited Paris, of which in its revolutionary phase he gives a lively picture, and received a promise of aid; Hoche, with whom he had an interview, being eager for the enterprise.

Among the people generally the rebellion was agrarian rather than religious, religious only as the Catholic peasantry believed that they saw in Protestantism a badge of general enmity. But that belief made the war between the sects internecine. It does not appear that any but a few of the lowest and coarsest of the priesthood took an active part in the rebellion. The order, as a whole, could hardly look with pleasure for the conquest of Ireland by[Pg 142] an atheist revolution. The French, in fact, had they become masters of Ireland for a time, would probably in the end have found themselves there, as in Spain, confronted by a hostile priesthood carrying with it the people.

In the extremity of danger, surrounded by gathering rebellion, Castle government had now to strike or fall. It struck, practically proclaiming martial law. But it was without the only safe means of military repression. Of regular soldiers it had few. Those few behaved well. Some of them earned by their conduct the blessings of the people. But in the main repression had to be entrusted to yeomanry and fencibles, little controlled by discipline, and infected, as a militia is always apt to be, and as in this case they were in an extreme degree, by the passions of the hour. These men, sent forth to disarm the people, in their search for concealed arms burned, slew, pitch-capped, flogged without stint or mercy, and turned a great district of the north and midland into a hell. The people retaliated with equal atrocity where they had the power. A large number of suspects were arbitrarily shipped on board the fleet, where it was believed they helped by their infection to beget the mutiny at the Nore. Lord Moira, a patriot Irish nobleman, protested[Pg 143] vehemently in the House of Lords, but his exaggeration and partiality broke the force of his appeal. To control the excesses of repression and restore military discipline, the gallant Abercrombie was put in command; but he lost his self-control, reviled the troops in an imprudent manifesto, broke with the government, and left matters worse than they had been before.

In Ulster, fraternities of strong Protestants, which had existed informally since 1689, were now formally organized as Orange Lodges. They embodied an intensely sectarian feeling and committed their share of outrages, but they lent the government powerful aid.

Conspicuous among the ruthless agents of repression was the head of the Beresfords, whose riding-house at Dublin was a daily scene of torture. Conspicuous also was Judkin Fitzgerald, the field of whose operations was Tipperary. Fitzgerald's apologists plead that his policy was successful. It might be so, but the cause of public order does not gain in the end by outraging that law of natural justice on respect for which public order must ultimately depend. Fitzgerald, savagely flogging a man on whom he had found a note in the French language, which not knowing French himself he[Pg 144] could not read, was presently assured by one who could read the note that it was perfectly harmless. He nevertheless continued the torture of the lash till the victim nearly expired. Such a case seems to defy apology. Fitzgerald, however, was not only protected from question by an Act of Indemnity, but rewarded with a title. On both sides all hearts were fired with the satanic madness of civil war.

French aid had been promised. To the unspeakable discredit of the British admiralty, it came. An expedition which had long been in preparation under Hoche was allowed to sail from Brest and unopposed to make the coast of Ireland at Bantry Bay. A storm which prevented a landing, the bad seamanship of the French, whose naval service had been shattered by the revolution, and the separation of the frigate which had the general on board from the rest of the fleet, saved Ireland from temporary conquest and Great Britain from the consequences of that disaster. It is remarkable that the peasantry in the neighbourhood of Bantry Bay received the soldiers of the government well and shared their potatoes with them. Was this loyalty or fear? Had the French landed, would the potatoes have been still more hospitably shared?[Pg 145] An expedition afterwards fitted out in Holland, now a vassal of France, at the very crisis of the mutiny at the Nore, was weatherbound till the mutiny was over and was then crushed by Duncan at Camperdown. A small French force under Humbert afterwards landed, and at Castlebar put the militia to shameful flight. But it was presently surrounded by superior numbers and forced to surrender. There were still some faint demonstrations, in one of which the arch-enemy of England, Wolfe Tone, met his doom. He imprudently betrayed his identity to his captors. His French commission availed him not. He escaped the gallows by suicide. He was a genuine enthusiast, and he was at all events on one of the only two practicable lines of action. Separation was the sole alternative to union. But had Tone got the upper hand, with his fanaticism and a savage peasantry thirsting for Protestant and English blood at his back, the political millennium in Ireland, as in France, would have opened with a reign of terror.

Disappointed of aid from France, the rebellion took the field by itself. There was a great rising in Wexford, headed by Father Murphy, a fighting priest, a compound of Wat Tyler and John Ball, who gave himself out as a supernatural personage,[Pg 146] and persuaded the people that he could catch bullets in his hands. The father showed a natural genius for war. His peasants fought desperately, and the Irish pike proved a formidable weapon in their hands. The rebels gained one or two successes in the field, and took the city of Wexford. They perpetrated fiendish cruelties. At Scullabogue they burned or butchered a barn full of Protestants. At Wexford they dragged their prisoners to the bridge, stripped them naked, hoisted them up on the points of their pikes, and threw them into the river. At Vinegar Hill, a name of ghastly memory, the rebel headquarters, a batch of Protestants was every day brought out after a mock trial to be massacred. The people being here under priestly leadership, the character of a religious crusade was given to their warfare, and every Protestant was a mark for their murderous fury. On the other hand, Protestants in the north who at the outset had been revolutionary, seeing the rebellion assume the character of a Catholic crusade, passed to the side of government and repression. One or two men of property were forced into leadership by the rebels; otherwise property was entirely on the side of the government.

After Scullabogue, Wexford, and Vinegar Hill,[Pg 147] there could not fail to be a terrible outpouring of vengeance. It came in full measure, as we learn from the correspondence of Cornwallis, a soldier of high distinction and character, who was sent in place of Camden as viceroy to close the scene. He is much afraid, he says, that any man in a brown coat who is found within several miles of the field of action is butchered without discrimination. The Irish militia, he says, are totally without discipline, contemptible before the enemy when any serious resistance is made to them, but ferocious and cruel in the extreme when any poor wretches either with or without arms come within their power. In short, murder appears their favourite pastime. The conversation of the principal persons of the country all tends to encourage the system of blood, and the conversation even at his own table, where he does all he can to prevent it, always turns on shooting, burning, hanging. If a priest has been put to death, the greatest joy is expressed by the whole company. "Who fears to speak of '98?" said a patriot bard in other days. The answer is, every one who is not utterly lost to reason and humanity. These militia men, it is to be borne in mind, were Irish, not English, and their murderous enmity was the enmity of one section of Ireland to another.

[Pg 148]

XII

Pitt now resolved on a legislative union of Ireland with England and Scotland, thus reverting to the policy of the Commonwealth. But union had been the ideal of Molyneux, and since the revolution of 1782 it had found many advocates, among them Adam Smith. An Irish government of sectarian ascendancy and oligarchy combined, controlled, and held in precarious subordination to the government of Great Britain by intrigue and corruption, had ended in murderous and ruinous conflict of political parties, social classes, and religious sects. In its realm people had been refusing to eat pork because the swine might have fed on human flesh. Foreign invasion had been invited. It had come, and only by repeated miracles had Great Britain as well as Ireland been saved in the last extremity of peril. Nor had that peril ceased. It was much to be deplored that Pitt could not, like Cromwell and the Council of State, effect the union by simply calling

34

representatives of Ireland to the Parliament at Westminster. Situated as Pitt was, he had,[Pg 149] as Castlereagh laconically put it, "to buy the fee simple of Irish corruption." The price he paid was compensation in money to the owners of pocket boroughs and profuse grants of peerages. The process was not edifying. Cornwallis, who had come at once to put an end to havoc and to carry the union, having a strict sense of honour, might well recoil from his task. Bribery with money has not been brought home to the government, though in one case at least it has been brought home to the opposition. From that stain the union is free. A pretty large sum was needed to tune the press and for campaign expenses. Pocket boroughs in those days were deemed property, and had been so treated in Pitt's Reform Bill for England. The compensation paid the owners of boroughs was not above the market price, and it was paid to the opponents as well as to the supporters of the union; Lord Downshire, the most powerful opponent of the union, as it happened, receiving the largest sum of all. Foster, who made the greatest speech in Parliament against the union, received seventy-five hundred pounds for his half share of a pocket borough. In the absence of such compensation the owners of pocket boroughs and the purchasers of seats for them would have been virtually[Pg 150] bribed by their private interest apart from any political consideration to oppose the bill. Something was needed to induce a powerful and selfish oligarchy to part with the field of its ascendancy and its ambition. For that purpose the lavish creation of peerages was used. It cost the nation nothing, and titles which had been openly used as bribes were not capable of much degradation. Pitt is upbraided for not having taken the sense of the nation by means of a general election. The sense of a nation of which at least three-quarters were not eligible to Parliament! The sense of the proprietors of nomination boroughs on the question of depriving them of their property and its influence! The sense of a nation, the passions of which had not had time to cool after a furious civil war, a civil war the ashes of which still fiercely glowed and might by the excitement of a general election have been fanned again into a flame! It is ever to be lamented that the thing could not have been done in a simpler and less questionable way. But it had to be done. Venality was venal, and, its consent being necessary to the salvation of the state, had to be bought. The purity of Pitt's motives or of those of his colleagues cannot be questioned. The idea that he had provoked rebellion to make[Pg 151] way for union is a slander which only political frenzy could fabricate or believe.

What was the feeling in Ireland at large it is very hard to determine. There were addresses and declarations on both sides, but we cannot tell how they were got up. Cornwallis made a canvassing tour. His opinion at first was that Dublin was furiously opposed but the rest of the country was favourable. This estimate changed as the struggle went on. Dublin, of course, was the centre of excitement. At the outset it was the scene of a riot. The capital could not like to lose the seat of government and the social centre; nor could the Irish bar like the transfer of the supreme jurisdiction to Westminster, or the severance of the Parliamentary from the forensic career; the two, while Parliament sat in Dublin, having been habitually, and often brilliantly, combined. Cork, on the other hand, was flattered with the prospect of becoming a second Glasgow. It seems strange that the Orangemen should then have been against the union, of which they have since been the staunchest supporters. But they no doubt scented the approach, with the union, of Catholic emancipation. The Catholic hierarchy, headed by Archbishop Troy, was strongly for the union, and unquestionably[Pg 152] drew with it a large following both of clergy and laity. The hope was undoubtedly held out of Catholic emancipation, possibly accompanied by a provision for the Catholic priesthood, as a sequel to the union; though no positive pledge was or could be given. At the same time it is to be borne in mind that the general sympathy of a Catholic priesthood would be with the British government as the chief antagonist of an atheist France. The terrible tension of '98 had probably been followed in many quarters by collapse and readiness to acquiesce in anything that could hold out to life and property the protection of a strong government. The "Annual Register" for 1802 says that at the first election of Irish members to the United Parliament no supporter of the union lost his election or was even upbraided on that account; that in the county of Dublin alone did a candidate think his opposition to the union such a claim to popular favour as to make it worth his while to allude to it; and that some of the largest and most independent counties returned strong supporters of the union. Cornwallis reports that in Dublin, the chief centre of opposition, when at last the royal assent was given to the bill, not a murmur was heard nor, as he believed, was there[Pg 153] any expression of ill-humour throughout the whole city.

The Established Church of Ireland would be willing to support a measure which, by identifying it with the English establishment, converted it from the Church of a small minority into a limb of the Church of a great majority, thus giving it a tenable ground of existence and a pledge of support which it fondly hoped would never fail.

The campaign of opinion, at all events, was conducted on both sides with perfect freedom. There is no pretence for alleging that the union was carried by military force. The affair at Dublin was a street riot, for the repression of which it was necessary to call in the troops. Nothing like military terrorism in fact is alleged. Twelve months before the passing of the union, and in the middle of the struggle, Cornwallis said that "the force remaining in Ireland was sufficient to maintain peace, totally inadequate to repel foreign invasion."

There were historic debates in the Irish Parliament. Grand speeches were made in the nationalist and patriotic vein by opponents of the union. Grattan, the author of the constitution of 1782, came in his volunteer uniform to bedew its hearse with his oratoric tears. The dramatic effect was[Pg 154] enhanced by the bodily infirmity of the great patriot and orator, which obliged him to speak sitting. Plunket put forth to the utmost those powers of debate which led Lord Russell to pronounce him of all the many speakers whom he had heard the most convincing. Foster produced a profound effect by his mastery of commercial and financial detail, though in this part of the field he had to contend with the supreme and unclouded judgment of Adam Smith left on record in favour of union. As strong an argument as any was that Ireland would be in danger of losing her leading men, who would be drawn away to England. But absenteeism was already rife, and was likely to be in the main diminished rather than increased by any measure which made Ireland a happier abode. To the spirit of nationality telling appeals could not fail to be made; but to what the nationality amounted, whether it was nominal or real, of the heart or merely of local boundary, had with terrible clearness appeared. In the speeches of the opposition there seems to have been much more of political argument of a general kind and of patriotic sentiment than of reference to the actual working of the Constitution of 1782 and the consequences to which it had led.

[Pg 155]Of all the opponents of the union on the high patriotic ground, the most fervid was Plunket. "For my own part," he exclaimed, "I will resist it to the last gasp of my existence, and with the last drop of my blood, and when I feel the hour of my dissolution approaching I will, like the father of Hannibal, take my children to the altar and swear them to eternal hostility against the invaders of their country's freedom." It is to be hoped that Plunket's children, if they took the oath, found absolution; for the father soon afterwards, sitting in the united Parliament of which he was a distinguished member, had so far changed his sentiments as to say of the union; "As an Irishman I opposed that union; as an Irishman I avow that I did so openly and boldly, nor am I now ashamed of what I then did. But though in my resistance to it I had been prepared to go the length of any man, I am now equally prepared to do all in my power to render it close and indissoluble. One of the apprehensions on which my opposition was founded, I am happy to say, has been disappointed by the event. I had been afraid that the interest of Ireland, on the abolition of her separate legislature, would come to be discussed in a hostile Parliament. But I can now state—and I wish when[Pg 156] I speak that I could be heard by the whole of Ireland—that during the time that I have sat in the united Parliament I have found every question that related to the interests or security of that country entertained with indulgence and treated with the most deliberate regard."

Grattan too sat in the united Parliament enjoying a Nestorian dignity and at first, Parliamentary reformer though he was, for a nomination borough. He voted for one of those measures of coercion, the necessity for which unhappily soon made itself felt. The most telling speech of all against union in the Irish Parliament was that of Foster; and Foster too sat in the united Parliament, was reconciled to Pitt, was by him made chancellor of the Irish exchequer, and became a peer of the United Kingdom.

The cause of the union in debate was pleaded by Clare and Castlereagh, inferior to their opponents in eloquence, though Clare was a very formidable speaker as well as a very strong man.

Through the British Parliament the union was carried by overwhelming majorities, though opposed by Grey, who afterwards, as prime minister, became its firm upholder, and by Sheridan, far less sage than brilliant, while Fox refused to attend the[Pg 157] debates, throwing out a hint that he preferred something in the way of federation; what, he did not say. In the Irish Parliament at first the measure was defeated. It was carried at length by dead-lift effort on the part of Clare and Castlereagh, who, leading for the government, did unquestionably make unlimited and by no means scrupulous use of such expedients as in those days were more freely employed by governments to push vital measures through the House. That such expedients should have prevailed is to be deplored as a stain on the origin of the union. At the same time it proves the rottenness of the assembly then on trial for its life. Nor should it be forgotten that on the side of opposition to the union were arrayed purely local and personal interests not more respectable in themselves than were the methods by which their resistance was overcome.

36

Let Irish patriots, when they bewail the extinction of the independent Parliament of Ireland, remember that its last days had been marked by eager support of the most ruthless and sanguinary measures of repression.

No serious exception appears to have been taken to the political bargain which gave Ireland one hundred representatives in the House of Commons[Pg 158] and thirty-two representatives, including four bishops sitting by rotation, in the House of Lords. The party system has never been constitutionally recognized, and it was not observed that the representative peers, elected by their own order, would always be Tory, to the total exclusion of the other party. About the fiscal bargain questions are raised. These affect not the political issue.

Viceroyalty, with Castle executive, was retained. This may be said to be a relic of dependence. But the need of a separate administration unfortunately has never ceased. When, in 1850, it was moved to abolish the lord-lieutenancy, Ireland protested, and in deference to her veto the measure was withdrawn. Ireland retained her separate judiciary and for some time her separate department of finance.

It was in regard to the religious question that the union was for the time a failure. Pitt kept his word. He proposed Catholic emancipation to his cabinet and pressed it on the king. He was foiled by the rogue and sycophant Wedderburn, who for his personal ends played on the king's morbid conscience and was aided in his work by the influence of two archbishops, through whom a state church once more rendered its political[Pg 159] service to the nation. Pitt paid the debt of honour by resignation. It is said that if he had persevered he would have prevailed, and the king would have submitted, as he did in other cases, such as the acknowledgment of American independence, the dismissal of Thurlow, the permission to Lord Malmesbury to treat with France, the recall of the Duke of York, and the admission of Fox to the government. But not one of these was a case of religious conscience, nor in one of them had the king a great body of national sentiment on his side, as he had, and knew that he had, in his resistance to Catholic emancipation. He afterwards turned out the Grenville ministry, which proposed to admit Catholics to military command, and in so doing was manifestly sustained by the nation. After all, Pitt must have known best what could be done with the king. That his resignation was less of a sacrifice, because he thus escaped the necessity of treating for peace with France, is conjecture, and does not affect the actual propriety of his course. The king having in consequence of the excitement been threatened with a recurrence of his malady, Pitt waived the Catholic question for the king's lifetime, and, when called by the extreme need of the country, returned to power on that[Pg 160]understanding. He would have done little good, and not have gratified the nation by driving the king mad and transferring the government in the midst of the great war to the Prince of Wales as Regent and the revellers of Carlton House. In criticising the action of public men at this period, we must always bear in mind the overmastering exigencies of the war. Pitt, though he waived his principle on the subject of Catholic emancipation, never renounced it. It passed to his pupil Canning, and within a generation prevailed.

The only concession made at this time to the Catholics was the endowment of Maynooth as a seminary for the Catholic priesthood of Ireland, cut off from the seminaries of the continent by the war.

Since the union, there has been much that was deplorable in the state of Ireland and in the relations of the two islands, the main source of which, however, as will presently appear, was not political. There has been a hateful series of coercion acts. But there have been no Tudor hostings; there has been no 1641; no 1689; no 1798. No fleet of an invader has anchored in Bantry Bay. Belfast, once the seed-plot of revolution, has prospered and been content. Two years afterwards revolution[Pg 161] flamed up again for a moment in the abortive rising of Emmet. Then it died down, to break forth seriously, at least as civil war, no more.

The union must be taken to have been a union in the full sense of the term, putting an end to separate identity, not merely a standing contract between two parties, each of which retained the right of enforcing the contract against the other. On this understanding Parliament has acted, and is likely again to act in the case of the representation, as well as in the disestablishment of the Irish Church. The United Kingdom cannot be hide-bound forever by the terms which, necessarily having reference to the circumstances of its formation, must, like those circumstances, have been deemed liable to change.

It is unfortunate that no common name for the united nationality could be found. "British" excludes the Irish, "English" both the Irish and the Scotch, and separatist sentiment is fostered by the retention of the old national name.

Victory over the French Revolution and Napoleon was accompanied by an ascendancy of Toryism, which kept Liverpool at the head of the government for fourteen years. In this both islands fared alike. But the Cabinet was divided on the subject[Pg 162] of Catholic emancipation. Plunket, still a Liberal though now a Unionist, showed his power as a debater in the Catholic cause. Castlereagh and Canning were on the Liberal side. Emancipation was carried in the Commons, thrown out in the lords, while old Eldon drank to the thirty-nine peers who had saved the Thirty-nine Articles, little thinking how soon he was to be smitten in the house of his friends. On Liverpool's death there were a few months of Canning and a brief interlude of Goodrich. Then power reverted to the Tory and anti-Catholic section of the Liverpool combination, at the head of which were Wellington and Peel. Peel, in whom hereditary Toryism was combined with natural openness of mind and practical sagacity, as well as with supreme skill in administration, seemed specially sent to carry England safely by the bridge of Conservatism over the gulf between the old era and the new. He had been one of the anti-Catholic section of the Liverpool government, and in that character had been elected to Parliament by the clerical and then Protestant University of Oxford. But he had administered Ireland for six years; had seen the state of things there; had been impressed and shown symptoms of a change of sentiment. He[Pg 163] dealt liberally with Catholics in the matter of patronage. He and Wellington now acquiesced in the relief of the Dissenters by the repeal of the Test and Corporation Acts. Probably they were hesitating on the brink of Catholic emancipation when they were impelled by a new force. The Catholic cause had found for itself a first-rate leader, organizer, and orator, Daniel O'Connell.

[Pg 164]

XIII

Daniel O'Connell, whose figure fills the next page in Irish history, was a Dublin barrister who, having gained a unique reputation as a skilful or more than skilful winner of verdicts, passed from the forensic to the political field. He was of pure Irish blood, Irish in physiognomy, typically Irish in character. Nature had endowed him with all the gifts of a popular leader, bodily as well as mental; for he had a voice of unrivalled power and compass as well as extraordinary tact in dealing with the masses and skill in the conduct of agitation. His oratory was such as never failed to tell with his Irish audience, while its violent exaggeration, its disregard of truth and offensiveness of expression too often excited the just resentment of those whom he assailed and repelled all moderate and right-minded men. At the same time he knew how to play the courtier, as he showed when George IV. visited Ireland. He entered public life without the blessing of the veteran Grattan, who accused him of setting afloat the bad passions of the people,[Pg 165] venting calumny against Great Britain, and making politics a trade. That his motives were mixed is probable. But of his Irish patriotism there could be no doubt. O'Connell was a most devout Catholic, enjoyed the hearty confidence of the priesthood, and was able to make full use of its influence in calling out and marshalling the people. He thus opened a new era in the history of Irish agitation. In return, he supported the priesthood in its extreme pretensions; notably in defeating a proposal for the admission of Catholics to political power subject to securities for the loyalty of their Church which conflicted with high priestly pretensions, though it had been favourably entertained at Rome. It was on this point that he and Grattan broke. O'Connell, with the aid of his priestly fuglemen, formed a great Catholic association to overawe the government. On the other side, the Orangemen, now heartily Unionist, rushed to arms. A fierce conflict ensued in Ireland, with some danger to the peace. In the course of it the Duke of York, heir presumptive to the Crown, electrified the country and filled the heart of Eldon and true blue Protestantism with joy by a solemn declaration that if he became king he would veto Catholic emancipation. After trying his power[Pg 166] by carrying some elections, O'Connell determined to bring the conflict to a head by himself standing for Parliament in defiance of the law by which, as a Catholic, he was excluded. He carried his election for Clare against the candidate of the gentry by the votes of the Catholic peasantry, the forty-shilling freeholders; the influence of the Church with its sacraments being openly employed in his support. Peel and Wellington now gave way and carried the admission of the Catholics to Parliament, only tempering the shock to their Tory supporters by the abolition of the forty-shilling freehold; no great blow to liberty, since the only question was whether the forty-shilling freeholder should be the tool of the landlord or of the priest. The refusal to O'Connell of the rank of king's counsel, to which he had become eligible, was defended as another sop to the Tories; but it really was a mark of resentment, very unwise as well as undignified, though partly excused by the offensiveness of O'Connell's bearing and language. It may have been unwillingness to confess change of opinion that led Wellington and Peel to ascribe the concession of Catholic emancipation to fear of civil war. O'Connell could not have put into the field any force capable of making head against the forces of[Pg 167] the government, Ulster, the Orangemen, and the Irish gentry. He was himself utterly unwarlike, and there was no foreign power to come to his aid. The measure was a concession of right demanded not only by the Irish Catholics themselves, but by a large party in England which included the best intelligence of the country and the most powerful organs of the press, without the help of which it could not have been carried. Unhappily it was made to appear as a concession of fear.

O'Connell's victory made him the idol and the master of Catholic Ireland. A large revenue, called his "rent," was thenceforth raised for him by annual subscription. On this his enemies did not fail to reflect. He defended it as the necessary compensation for the sacrifice of a large professional income to the service of the country. At his ancestral mansion of Darrynane, on the wild, thoroughly Celtic, and Erse-speaking coast of Kerry, the "Liberator" held a rustic court profusely hospitable, amidst a circle of devoted adherents, with an open table at which as many as thirty guests were sometimes seated; thus presenting probably the nearest possible counterpart of the head of a great sept in the tribal days. To Darrynane a pilgrimage was made by Montalembert, who fondly hoped[Pg 168] that he had found in its master that union of devotion to the Church with liberty which was the ideal of the liberal Catholic school.

Would Catholic emancipation pacify Ireland? Its authors expected that it would. Even Macaulay appears to think that if the popular religion of Ireland had been treated at the union as the popular religion of Scotland was treated, all in Ireland, as in Scotland, might have been well. The result was disappointing. The Irish cotter had voted and shouted for Catholic emancipation at the bidding of the priests and the platform; but what he wanted and hoped to get by a revolution of any kind was, not so much political or religious change, as more oats and potatoes. His real grievances were hunger and nakedness. To afford those myriads a treacherous food, the behest of nature had been too much disregarded; lands destined for pasture had been turned into potato and oat plots. The millions, reduced to an animal existence, had gone on multiplying with animal recklessness. The increase was greater since rebellion and devastation were at an end. In this sense alone the consequences of the union may be said to have been evil. The priest enjoined marriage on moral grounds, perhaps not without an eye to fees. Between 1801[Pg 169] and 1841 population increased by three millions. More than ever, the homes were filthy hovels shared with swine, the beds litters of dirty straw, the dresses rags, the food the potato, while there was frequent dearth and sometimes famine. Eviction increased, since, the forty-shilling freehold franchise having been abolished, the landlord cared no longer to multiply holdings for the sake of votes. The land system, with its tiers of middlemen, was as cruel as ever. Tithe, the most odious of all imposts, was still collected in the most odious manner. As a consequence, peasant Ireland was still the scene of a vast agrarian war waged by a starving people against the landlord and the tithe-proctor. Arson, murder, carding and mutilation of middlemen and tithe-proctors were rife. Victims leaping from the windows of their burning houses were caught on pitchforks. The nation was undergoing a baptism of lawlessness and savagery. All the peasants were in the league of crime and screened the assassin. Law was powerless. Prosecution was hopeless. Murder was committed in open day and before a number of witnesses, all of whom, if brought into court, would perjure themselves in the common cause. A deep impression had been made upon Peel by the horrors of the agrarian[Pg 170] war. He had been particularly moved by a case showing the transcendent height which social passion had attained. A party of Whiteboys entered a house in which there were the man whom they came to murder, his wife, and their little girl. The man was in a room on the ground floor. His wife and their little girl were in a room above, with a closet, through a hole in the door of which the room could be seen. The woman heard the Whiteboys enter and knew their errand. She put the child into the closet, saying to her, "They are murdering your father below, then they will come up and murder me. Mind you look well at them and swear to them when you see them in court." The child obeyed. She looked on while her mother was murdered. She swore to the murderers in court, and they were hanged upon her evidence.

The evil had reached such a height that society in Ireland was almost on the point of dissolution. Ordinary coercion acts, of which there had been a series, failed and the Liberal government of Grey was compelled to have recourse to martial law.

The tide of reform, however, which began to flow in 1830, before it ebbed, brought to Ireland, besides her share in reform of the Parliamentary representation, the opening of the municipal councils,[Pg 171] which had been universally close and corrupt, and after Catholic emancipation still excluded Catholics. It brought commutation of tithe, a measure of immense value, far too long delayed, which shifted the burden of payment from the shoulders of the cotter to those of the landlord. It brought a poor law, cruelly needed in the midst of multiplying evictions. Furthermore, it brought in 1831-1833 the momentous gift of public education, national and undenominational, in the inauguration of which the Anglican primate, Archbishop Whateley, reconciling his advanced liberalism with his anomalous position, took a leading part. Ireland thus in national education preceded England by many years. Whateley had fellow-workers in liberal Catholics, ecclesiastical as well as lay, but the weight of Roman authority and influence was, as it always has been, and still is, against free education. The State Church of the minority succeeded in repelling attack; but it underwent some internal reform, including the suppression of ten superfluous bishoprics; a sacrilegious act of the state which helped to give birth to sacerdotal reaction at Oxford. After the abolition of the tithe-proctor, the State Church had become less odious to the people. The Castle administration was growing more[Pg 172] liberal. Lords-lieutenant tried to be fair in distribution of patronage. A Liberal secretary, a man of mark, Drummond, warned the Irish landlords that property had its duties as well as its rights. Peel, as Irish secretary, had laid the foundation of the Irish constabulary, that noble force of law and order which combines independent intelligence with the discipline of the regular soldier. Drummond rendered a most important service by completing the institution. The Irish constabulary has naturally in the main been composed of Protestants. But the Catholic policeman in Ireland has in a marked way resisted seditious influence and been true to the government and his duty. The Irishman follows his commander. Attempts to seduce Irish soldiers from fidelity to the colours seem to have generally failed.

O'Connell, with his following, helped to carry the Parliamentary Reform Bill of 1832, which, in fact, could not have been carried without their vote. He lent a general though not hearty or unwavering support to the Whig ministry of Grey, which, though it paid him some deference, was too strong to be under his control. But on the passing of a drastic coercion bill directed against political as well as agrarian disturbance, there was an angry rupture,[Pg 173] and the Whigs became "base, bloody, and brutal," like all others who crossed O'Connell's will. O'Connell was not handsomely treated. His eminence as a lawyer, combined with his influence in Ireland, entitled him to a high place. But his blustering violence, his unmeasured vituperation, his venomous abuse of England, and the changefulness of his moods made him a dangerous ally for any government. Cobden said, "O'Connell always treated me with friendly attention, but I never shook hands with him or faced his smile without a feeling of insecurity; and as for trusting him on any public question where his vanity or passions might interpose, I should have as soon thought of an alliance with an Ashantee chief."

The Melbourne and Russell ministry was weak and fain to lean on O'Connell with his Irish brigade for support and to allow him a voice in appointments, though it suffered greatly in English eyes by the alliance. O'Connell shouted with joy when that government was snatched from death and restored to a feeble existence by the refusal of the queen to change her bed-chamber women on Peel's demand. But the advent of Peel to power, with a strong government, filled him with rage and despair. The two men had quarrelled in Ireland, a challenge[Pg 174] had passed between them, and Peel was the object of O'Connell's bitterest hatred. In principle the new government was hostile to O'Connell, and its strength placed it wholly beyond his influence. His power was threatened with extinction. His rent, moreover, since there had been a lull in agitation, was rapidly falling off, and he was in pecuniary distress. The last, some think, was not his least urgent motive for embarking in another agitation. This time it was for a repeal of the union, of which he had before only thrown out fitful hints. He now raised the standard of repeal and issued his mandate to the priesthood to call out the peasantry in that cause. The priesthood joyfully obeyed. Monster meetings were held and were addressed by O'Connell in his most violent strain, with ostensible respect for constitutional methods, but with constant appeals to national hatred and suggestions of military force. The priests consecrated the meetings and the sentiments, celebrating Mass on the grounds. It is surely idle to contend that a priesthood acting thus and having its centre in Rome is only a Christian ministry, not a power of political disturbance. An outbreak appeared to be at hand, when the government took direct issue with the agitator by proclaiming a monster meeting[Pg 175] which he had appointed to be held at Clontarf; a scene suggestive of military force as it had been the field of the great Irish victory. O'Connell, who, if he was not pacific, was unwarlike, shrank from the conflict and called off the meeting. The government followed up the blow by indicting the agitator for sedition. There was a monster trial at Dublin, in the course of which, to preserve the Irish character of the scene, the attorney-general challenged the counsel on the other side to a duel. O'Connell was found guilty, but the verdict was afterwards quashed on appeal to the House of Lords, for irregularity in the panel, by the judgment of three Whigs against one Tory and the independent Brougham, though it had been upheld by seven of the nine judges to whom the case was referred. O'Connell was set free. But the spell of his ascendancy had been broken. By shrinking from the appeal to force he had forfeited the respect of the fighting section of his party. The Conservative government was invincibly strong. O'Connell's health and physical force had broken down. Thus ended the great Liberator's career. He bequeathed his body to Ireland and his heart to Rome. There can be no question about his devotion to either, whatever motives may have mingled with his devotion[Pg 176] to Ireland. Whether he did more good to the Irish cause by his patriotism than harm by the passions which he excited and the enmities he created, is a question about which different opinions have been formed. His blind attachment to the Church, had he been victorious, would have put Ireland under the control of a reactionary priesthood.

For some time before his death, O'Connell, by shrinking from force, had been losing the hearts and the adherence of a party of force on his own side called "Young Ireland," a set of young men, some highly gifted as journalists or poets, whose aim was not repeal but national independence, and who in their organ, *The Nation*, preached rebellion and revelled in the memory of '98.

Peel, victorious, graced his victory by concession, to which indeed he was heartily inclined. He saw that "Ireland was his difficulty," and wanted to treat the problem as liberally as his following of Protestants and squires would let him. He increased the grant to Maynooth, thereby constraining Gladstone, by way of satisfaction to his former self, to go through the form of resignation. He enabled the Catholic Church freely to receive charitable bequests. Not venturing to throw open[Pg 177] the fellowships and scholarships of Trinity College to the Catholics, he founded for their special benefit three undenominational colleges at Belfast, Cork, and Galway, forming together a university with power of granting degrees. This measure, excellent in its way, was but a partial success. The priesthood looked with invincible suspicion on free science, while Catholic professors of science, whom the Church might have trusted, were hardly to be found. But Peel touched the real root of the evil, and pointed to effective reform, when, in 1843, he issued a Commission of Inquiry into land occupancy in Ireland and the condition of the peasant occupants. The commission reported that the agricultural labourer of Ireland continued to suffer the greatest privations and hardships; that he was still dependent upon casual and precarious employment for subsistence; that he was still badly housed, badly clothed, and badly fed; and that he was undergoing sufferings greater than those of the people of any other country in Europe. Some tentative motions followed, but there had scarcely been time for the report of the commission to work, when the sentence of nature was pronounced with awful distinctness in the form of a great famine with pestilence in its train. The population of[Pg 178] Ireland at this time was probably double that which the island could happily bear. A precarious subsistence was afforded by the potato, which, always treacherous, now suddenly and completely failed. Peel, warned of impending calamity, at once opened the ports for the importation of grain, then grasped the occasion for the repeal of the Corn Laws, on the policy of which his own mind had been undergoing change. His administrative power and that of his colleagues would probably have done all that was possible to meet and mitigate the disaster. But at the critical moment his government was struck down by a conspiracy of Russell and the Whigs with the ire of the Corn Law squires and the vengeful ambition of Disraeli. Russell, who took his place, was far more an adept in party strategy than a master of practical administration. There ensued a heartrending scene, the climax of seven centuries of evil accident, maladministration, and Irish woe.

"Famine advances on us with giant strides," wrote an official in the August of 1846. "Towards the end of August," says Mr. T. P. O'Connor, "the calamity began to be universal and its symptoms to be seen. Some of the people rushed into the towns, others wandered along the highroads in the[Pg 179] vague hope of food. They plucked turnips from the fields, were glad to live for weeks on a single meal of cabbage a day, feasted on the dead bodies of horses and asses and dogs. There was a story of a mother eating the limbs of her dead child. Dead bodies were discovered with grass in their mouths and in their bowels; weeds were sought after with desperate eagerness; seaweed was greedily devoured; so were diseased cattle and diseased potatoes. Despair fell on all hearts and faces. The ties of kindred in some cases failed, parents neglecting their children and children turning out their aged parents. On the other hand, there were stories of parents dying of starvation to save a small store for their children. The workhouses, usually shunned, were overcrowded. In one, three thousand persons sought relief in a single day. They crowded even into the jails. Driven from the workhouses, people began to die by the roadside or alone in their despair within their cabins. Roads and streets were strewn with corpses. One inspector buried one hundred and forty bodies found on the highway. The scenes inside the cabins were even more horrible; husbands lay for a week in the same hovels with the bodies of their wives and children. The decencies[Pg 180]of burial were no longer observed. Then came the plague, attacking bodies already weakened by hunger." "A terrible apathy," says an eye-witness, "hangs over the poor of Skibbereen; starvation has destroyed every generous sympathy; despair has made them hardened and insensible, and they sullenly await their doom with indifference and without fear. Death is in every hovel; disease and famine, its dread precursors, have fastened on the young and the old, the strong and the feeble, the mother and the infant; whole families lie together on the damp floor devoured by fever, without a human being to wet their burning lips or raise their languid heads; the husband dies by the side of the wife, and she knows not that he is beyond the reach of earthly suffering; the same rag covers festering remains of mortality and the skeleton forms of the living, who are unconscious of the horrible contiguity; rats devour the corpse, and there is no energy among the living to scare them from their horrid banquet; fathers bury their children without a sigh, and cover them in shallow graves, round which no weeping mother, no sympathizing friends are grouped; one scanty funeral is followed by another and another. Without food or fuel, bed or bedding, whole families are shut[Pg 181] up in naked hovels, dropping one by one into the arms of death."[3]

All the devices of government by relief work and in other ways to grapple with the twofold calamity were palliatives and little more. The most effective measure of relief was a vast emigration to the United States and Canada, which also had its horrors. Thousands, already weakened by hunger and suffering, succumbed to the hardships of the passage; another multitude died on landing. Canada did all she could for the hapless strangers cast upon her shore. But ship-fever followed the fugitives, and graveyards were filled with their dead. It was reckoned that more than two hundred thousand persons died on the voyage or on arrival at their destination. Few Irishmen, however prejudiced against England, will deny that the people of Great Britain and Canada showed unbounded sympathy with Ireland in her affliction, and did their utmost for her relief. O'Connell himself, while he criticised the measures of the government, allowed that individual humanity and charity were abundant; that the noblest generosity was evinced by multitudes of the English; and that if individual generosity could save a nation, British[Pg 182] generosity would do it. He said that he was afraid of not finding words sufficient to express his strong and lively sense of English humanity. To charges of English indifference to Irish suffering, his words are a sufficient answer.

Close upon the famine and pestilence came 1848, the year of European revolution. Young Ireland, the party of force, did not fail to catch the flame. Its organ, *The Nation*, cried, "It is a death struggle now between the murderer and his victim. Strike! Rise, men of Ireland, since Providence so wills it! Rise in your cities and in your fields, on your hills, in your valleys, by your dark mountain passes, by your rivers and lakes and ocean-washed shores! Rise as a nation!" *The Irish Felon*, a journal still more advanced, was even more openly for war. But neither in city or field, on mountain or in valley, by pass or shore, did the people rise at the impassioned call. Young Ireland found at once that it was but a knot of literary men whose appeals to national feeling, penned as they were with vigour, might be read with sentimental pleasure but would rouse nobody to arms. O'Connell's mastery of the people depended on the support of the priesthood, given in a cause originally religious to that zealous champion of the Church who, dying, bequeathed[Pg 183] his heart to Rome. Young Ireland was more revolutionary than Catholic, as the priests did not fail to perceive. The desire of political revolution, apart from agrarianism, was not strong enough to rouse the peasantry to arms, though they had learned to hate England as the supposed source of their sufferings. The people, moreover, had hardly recovered from the depression caused by the famine. Young Ireland however raised its flag. Smith O'Brien, with a small party, made a trial trip, appealing to the people of two or three places, but met with no response. A farcical encounter with the police at the house of widow Cormack on the bog of Boulagh, followed by the capture of Smith O'Brien, was the end. The sentence of death passed on the leader of the revolt was wisely commuted by the government.

The famine had at least one good effect. It drew attention to the main source of the evil in Ireland, which was agrarian and social, not political and religious. But now it was supposed that the mischief lay in the inability of the landlords, overwhelmed with debt, burdened with family settlements, and crushed by the demands of the Poor Law, to perform their duty to their tenants. To remedy this evil was created the Encumbered Estates Court, with power to order the sale of[Pg 184] encumbered property on the petition of the creditors and give a clear title to the purchaser. The policy seemed sound, yet the result was not good. The court cleared out the old proprietors who lacked means to do their duty; it put in their place a new class of proprietors who, having been induced to buy the land on pure speculation, felt that they had no duty to do, and who, unlike their predecessors, had no kindly tie to the people. The new owners naturally proceeded to make the most of their purchase; and the way to make the most of their purchase clearly was to sweep out the cotter tenants and throw the land into large holdings. This some of them proceeded to do, and the consequence was a period of evictions almost vying in cruelty with the famine. Whole districts were cleared and relet in large holdings. Cabins were being thrown down in all directions. A thousand of them were levelled in one union within a few months, and the inmates were cast out helpless, half-naked, starving, to go to the union or perish. The cabins were burned that the people might not return to them. The suffering and misery, says a reporter, attendant upon these wholesale evictions, is indescribable. The number of houseless paupers in one union is beyond his calculation. Those evicted crowd [Pg 185]neighbouring cabins and villages, and disease is necessarily generated. In April he calculates that six thousand houses have been levelled since November, and he expects five hundred more by July. Wretched hovels had been pulled down, the inmates of which in a helpless state of fever and nakedness were left by the roadside for days. While inspecting a stone-breaking depot, the reporter observes one of the men take off his remnant of a pair of shoes and start across the fields. He follows him with his eye, and at a distance sees the blaze of a fire in the bog. He sends to inquire the cause of it and of the man's running from his work, and is told that the man's house had been levelled the day before, that he had erected a temporary hut, and that while his wife and children were gathering shell-fish on the beach and he was stone-breaking the bailiff fired it. This incident was one of several which made a deep impression on Peel, who would probably have moved with effect had he remained in power. Pages are filled with pictures of this kind. Civilized Europe could show nothing like it. It was almost enough to break forever the spirit of the nation, certainly to implant the bitterest memories, and here the main cause was misgovernment and bad law.

[Pg 186]Relief works were no cure, nor were they in themselves very rational, since the people, unfed, half-clothed, and living in pestilential mud-holes, were really too weak to work. Parliament so far interfered as to pass an act requiring forty-eight hours' notice of eviction to the relieving officers, prohibiting evictions two hours before sunset or sunrise, and on Christmas Day and Good Friday, and prohibiting the demolition of the house of a tenant about to be evicted. But this rather throws a lurid light on the state of things than effects a cure. The public even might have some reason to complain of the land-owner who recklessly cast upon the poor rates or upon public charity the human encumbrances of his land.

Apart from overpopulation and its effects, the Irish land-law unquestionably needed reform. The people, struggling with each other for their sole means of subsistence, undertook to pay exorbitant rents, and their improvements, if they made any, became without compensation the property of the landlord. In Ulster, always exceptional, there prevailed a certain measure of tenant-right, something like the English copyhold. In Ireland the demand for tenant-right now began to be loudly heard. An English Radical, Sharman Crawford, brought [Pg 187]forward a measure in Parliament, but without effect. For some years nothing effectual was done in the way of reform. Palmerston, to whom power passed, though in foreign policy he dallied with revolution, was conservative, especially on social subjects, at home. "Tenant's right is landlord's wrong" was his judgment on the agrarian question. On the Irish side there was no leader of worth or force. Patriotism was in a trance, and the chronicler of the Nationalist party indignantly proclaims that the cause was betrayed by a series of low adventurers who embraced it as the way to preferment. "The most common type of Irish politician," he says in his anguish, "in these days was the man who entered Parliamentary life solely for the purpose of selling himself for place and salary." "This," he adds, "was the golden season, when every Irishman who could scrape as much money together as would pay his election expenses was able after a while to obtain a governorship or some other of the many substantial rewards which English party leaders were able to give to their followers." The constituencies, it seems, political feeling being at a low ebb, were ready to elect the man who could bring them public pelf. Of the adventurers, the worst was Sadleir, who, with his set, attempted to[Pg 188]intrigue with the Peelites, and who, being a financial swindler as well as a political schemer, became bankrupt and committed suicide. So the cause of the Three F's—Fixity of tenure, Free sale, and Fair rents—made no way. English Radicals in Parliament stood all the time ready to move with the Irish on this question or for Disestablishment; but the Irish members were taken up with intriguing for places for themselves, for appointments of the sons of their constituents to clerkships in Somerset House, or for a government subsidy to the Galway Packet contract. Irish writers are bound to remember that Englishmen were not responsible for the choice or character of Irish members. They are bound also to remember the impression which the members chosen by the Irish could not fail to make on English minds. The British Parliament could not justly be said to be "deaf, blind, and insolently ignorant," though it was not on the right track. It might be excused for being a little deaf and blind to the appeals of "a motley gang of as disreputable and needy adventurers as ever trafficked in the blood and tears of a nation."

From the time of the union to this time there had been, and long after this time continued to be,[Pg 189] a series of coercion acts, rendered necessary by agrarian outrage. There were thirty-two enactments of this kind between the union and 1844. It would have been almost better, had it been possible, frankly to suspend the constitution while the true remedy was being applied.

Liberal leadership now devolved from Palmerston on Gladstone, thus bringing on the political field a new and immensely powerful motive power. Gladstone was in opposition. In his mind a natural, and under the party system legitimate, desire of recovering power for his party and himself perhaps mingled with a sincere though tardily formed conviction of the injustice of such an institution as the State Church of a small minority in Ireland. It was unfortunate that he, like Peel and Wellington, gave fear of Irish violence as a motive for doing justice. After some premonitory hints, he, in former days the great champion of state religion, declared for disestablishment. His case was overwhelmingly strong. Faint and feeble were the arguments on the other side. The institution was an anachronism, an anomaly, and a scandal. Its past had been miserable. It had made no converts; it had made many rebels. By its tests and its intolerance it had divided the Protestant interest, sending many[Pg 190] a Presbyterian across the sea to fight for the American Revolution. Its ministry had been jobbed, its character defiled, by unscrupulous politicians. Of late, however, it had been greatly reforming itself, and it had got rid of its tithe-proctors by the commutation of tithes. Its clergy generally were now on friendly terms with the people. Its last hour was by far its best. Vested interests were respected in the change, and the unblest establishment glided quietly and safely into its new and happier life as a purely spiritual church. Through the Commons the measure passed with ease; through the Lords, like other great measures of change, it was forced by fear.

[Pg 191]

XIV

From disestablishment of the Church Gladstone, now in the full swing of his Liberalism, proceeded next year to reform the land system of Ireland. Taking his cue from Ulster tenant-right, perhaps also from English copyhold, he passed an act, the first of a series which, by giving compensation for improvements and for disturbance, restricting eviction, regulating rents, and furnishing to the tenant by government loans the means of purchasing the fee, has gone far towards transferring the ownership from the landlord to the tenant. Some of these measures have virtually involved confiscation, notably in the case of purchasers under the Encumbered Estates Act, to whom full ownership had been morally guaranteed.

Economically, the tendency, indeed the aim, of the land acts has been to make Ireland a land of peasant proprietors. The social tendency of such legislation is to the abolition of the gentry, of the value of whose leadership to a people eminently in need of leaders, Gladstone, personally[Pg 192] ignorant of Ireland, might not be a competent judge. Unquestionably, the relations between landlord and tenant called for reform. The appropriation of the tenant's improvements by the landlord was in itself plainly unjust, and the sweeping evictions yielded in cruelty only to the famine. But for overpopulation the immediate remedy was depletion. Had Gladstone said that the overpopulation was originally the consequence of misgovernment and repression of industry which, reducing the people to abject misery, had wrecked their self-respect and self-restraint, he would have been emphatically right, and the fact cannot be too constantly kept in mind. Gladstone might also have said with truth that emigration was a mournful cure, though it transferred the emigrant to a far happier land and lot. But the overpopulation having taken place, whatever the cause, the only remedy was depletion. No expansion of manufacturing industry, commerce, or mining adequate to the absorption of the surplus population could be expected in time to meet the pressing call for relief. Irishmen are sensitive on this point, but no disparagement of the Irish race is implied in the recognition of the facts. Overpopulation was not the fault of the people, but their misfortune. There[Pg 193] has been a very large migration of the Irish into England and Scotland as well as into the United States.

Gladstone's measure, however, fell short of Irish expectation, which was the three F's: Fixity of tenure; Fair rent; Freedom of sale. A land war presently broke out and became combined with a struggle nominally for Home Rule, really for separation from Great Britain. The political part of this agitation, rebellion as it really was, had its main source and support, not in Ireland, but in the Irish population of the United States. Even before the famine there had been an emigration of Irish to America, so large as by its political effects to alarm American patriotism and give birth to the great Know-nothing Movement in defence of American nationality. The Irish, being highly gregarious and unused to large farming, settled in cities. When they went out to work on railways or canals, it was in large gangs. They were drawn into the vortex of politics and became the retainers of crafty politicians, who, in secret, smiled at their simplicity. They fell almost invariably into the Democratic party. The name may have attracted them; but the Democratic party was that of the Southern slave-owner, who was glad to enlist the Irishman[Pg 194] as his humble ally at the North and to pay him out of the treasury of political corruption. The rank and file of Tammany were largely Irish. O'Connell had been nobly hostile to slavery. His kinsmen and admirers on the other side of the Atlantic were, on the contrary, vehement supporters of slavery, and jealous assertors of their superiority over the enslaved race. Such is the tendency of the newly enfranchised. In the war between the North and the South the Irish in New York rose against the draft and committed great outrages, especially against the negro, among other things setting fire to a negro orphan asylum. They were ruthlessly put down. After

44

the famine, emigration greatly increased. Family affection among the Irish is beautifully strong, and the members of a family who had gone before sent home their earnings to pay for the passage of those whom they had left behind. It has been reckoned that the Irish have expended twenty millions sterling in this way. With a passionate love of Ireland the American Irish combined a still more passionate hatred of England as Ireland's tyrant and oppressor. Invasion and destruction of England were their dream. Always addicted to secret fraternities and natural adepts in conspiracy, they formed associations for[Pg 195] war on England; that of the Fenians and that of the still more rabid and bloodthirsty Clan-na-Gael, whose utterances were frenzies of hatred. Large sums were subscribed; Irish servant-girls, with a patriotism which in any case was honourable to them, giving freely of their wages. American politicians flattered the mania, and harvested the Irish vote. The war bequeathed to the Fenians some regular soldiers, among others, Mitchel, who had been conspicuous in the ranks of slavery. The Fenians invaded Canada and overthrew a corps of Canadian volunteers, but retired on the approach of regulars; a bad omen for their conquest of England. Conquest of England the Fenians did not attempt, beyond a farcical essay at Chester. But they helped greatly to kindle rebellion in Ireland, to provide it with money, and to supply it with assassins. The National League, the form which, in Ireland, political combined with agrarian rebellion assumed, almost ousted the law and the queen's government. It resisted the payment of rents. Those who opposed its will were "boycotted," a term of which this is the origin. Sometimes they were murdered. A stripling was murdered for having served a master who had come under the ban of the League. A wife was mobbed on her[Pg 196] way home from viewing the body of her murdered husband. Lord Frederick Cavendish, the Irish secretary, going to Ireland with the kindest intentions, and the permanent secretary, Mr. Burke, were stabbed to death in the Phœnix Park. Mr. W. E. Forster, distinguished by his humane efforts at the time of the famine, was marked for assassination. At the outbreak of the rebellion a policeman escorting Fenian prisoners had been murdered at Manchester, and an attempt made to blow up Clerkenwell Prison, where a Fenian was confined, had caused the deaths of twelve people and the maiming of one hundred and twenty. Gladstone had made the mistake of treating the alarm caused by those outrages as a motive for doing justice to Ireland. The motive for doing justice to Ireland was justice.

The assassination of Cavendish and Burke, it is right to say, was the act, not of the Land League or of any conspiracy in Ireland itself, but of the Invincibles, a club of frenzied Irish in the United States. By the Irish leaders it was heartily condemned. That it was regarded with utter abhorrence in the Irish quarters of English cities was denied by observers at the time. Fierce and blind were the passions of those days.

[Pg 197]To repress what was in fact a rebellion fed by foreign aid, to uphold the law, and rescue life and industry in Ireland from the lawless tyranny of the National League, as it was called, the government, as was its plain duty, sought and obtained extraordinary powers, and threw a number of the leaders of the rebellion into prison. It was time, when loyal citizens were joining the League for protection in their callings, which the queen's government could no longer afford. When the Irish rose against the draft in New York, the Americans shot down several hundreds of them without process of law.

In the British Parliament the "rebel" party, as Bright justly called it, had found a leader of mark in Parnell, a man of great ability and force of character, incisive and forcible, if not eloquent, as a speaker. He had supplanted in the leadership Mr. Butt, a man of social sensibility and refinement, unfitted for an aggressive part. The agitation under Parnell combined agrarianism with repeal, thus giving the political part of the movement a hold upon the people and a force and a formidable extension in Ireland which by itself it had never had. The Land League, becoming the National League, almost supplanted the queen's government in Ireland.

Parnell's avowed aim was the foundation of a[Pg 198] peasant proprietorship. Neither he nor any of his party seem to have cared to study dispassionately the natural aptitudes of the country, and to satisfy themselves whether it was capable of supporting the population which disastrous events and sinister influences had accumulated upon it. Their main object was political. It was, under the guise of repealing the union, to sever Ireland from Great Britain. As an inducement to the peasantry to support them in that attempt, they offered to transfer the property in the land from the landlord to the tenant, though with a decorous promise of indemnity. Mr. Parnell's name was English, and he had been educated at Cambridge. It was understood that his bearing towards his Celtic associates was high and that he was peremptory as well as absolute in command. At his side was Mr. Biggar, whose great gift was unparalleled effrontery. The two undertook to coerce the British Parliament by obstruction. Had the British Parliament been itself, it would quickly have asserted its dignity. But it was split into factions, upon the balance of which Parnell and Biggar were able to play. Gladstone succumbed so far as by an equivocal agreement, nicknamed the Kilmainham Treaty, to release Parnell and his associates from prison. On the other hand, the[Pg 199] Conservatives coming into power struck the flag of the law by refusing to renew the Crimes Act for the protection of loyalty in Ireland, while they angled for the Parnellite vote by casting reproach on the conduct of a lord-lieutenant who had done his duty.

At the general election which followed, Gladstone went to the country, appealing for a majority which should enable him to settle the Irish question independently of Parnell. Parnell passed the word to all his partisans, both in Ireland and in the Irish quarters of English towns, to vote against the Liberals. They obeyed. Gladstone was defeated. Then he who had denounced Parnell as wading through rapine to dismemberment; who had proclaimed his arrest as a rebel to an applauding multitude at Guildhall; who had thrown him and scores of his followers into prison; who had never given to the nation a hint of his sympathy with Parnell's agitation, suddenly turned round and coalesced with Parnell. He put forth an apology for his conversion founded on the hidden workings of his own mind. But what availed the workings of his own mind if all the time he was carrying on the policy of repression, misleading the nation thereby? It is true he might have pointed to the coquetting of the[Pg 200] other party, or its leaders, with the Parnellites. He might perhaps with more force have appealed to his own unquestionably sincere sympathy with all who were struggling for independence. His retrospective imagination was strong, and having changed so much he had always present to his mind the possibility of further change. It made his language sometimes capable of unforeseen interpretation.

The Liberal party was filled with astonishment, confusion, and dismay. But the *Times* stood fast and rallied the adherents of the union. To the steadfastness and power of this great journal the defeat of Gladstone's policy and the salvation of the union were largely due. Bright's refusal to cast in his lot with the "rebel" party was also a heavy blow to Gladstone. The political connection between the two men had been growing close, and Bright might almost be said to personify justice to Ireland, as to all the weak and oppressed. If there was a man who would have protested against the sacrifice of Ireland to English interests it was John Bright. Lord Hartington presented himself with unexpected vigour as a Unionist leader. Gladstone was defeated in the House of Commons and still more signally in the general election which followed, Conservative and Unionist Liberals voting[Pg 201] together on the special issue. In the contest Gladstone lashed himself into fury, appealed to Separatist sentiment, not in Ireland only, but in Scotland and Wales, to the prejudice of the masses against the classes, of the uneducated against the educated and the learned professions. He was fired with enthusiasm for the right. His instincts were always high. But this did not make him a cool-headed statesman warily dealing with a question which touched the life of the commonwealth.

Now fortune played a strange trick. Parnell, the leader and mainstay of the League, Gladstone's ally, was convicted of adultery. Adultery is not political, but it was too much both for the Irish hierarchy and for the nonconformist conscience. Parnell had to be dragged from the helm of the Irish party, to which he clung with a frantic tenacity, such as proved him after all to be, though a very remarkable, hardly a very great, man.

Raised once more by another turn of fortune's wheel in the party game to power, Gladstone again brought forward a Home Rule Bill. This time he, with the help of the Irish members, pushed the bill through the House, partly by closure, in a form already condemned by himself, giving Ireland a separate Parliament for her own affairs, and at the[Pg 202] same time retaining her representation in the British Parliament, with power there to vote upon all questions. The Irish delegation would have played, as in fact it does now, for its own purposes, on the balance of British parties, and baffled any attempt to enforce restrictions on the doings of its own Parliament which the Home Rule Act might have imposed. The majority for the bill in the Commons was forty-three, including eighty Irish members. British members of the House of Commons who voted for the bill probably reckoned on its being killed in the Lords. Killed it was there with a vengeance. Gladstone appealed to the people against the Lords, but in vain. Thus ended in disaster his wonderful career. His speeches on Home Rule showed, like all his speeches, vast oratorical power, mastery of details, clearness and liveliness in exposition. But weak points are also apparent. The Irish Parliament cannot have been at once a sink of corruption and an institution with which it was sacrilege to interfere. The comparison of the union in criminality to the massacre of St. Bartholomew must surely have made all hearers but the Irish smile. Upon this subject the speaker raves, and generally he forgets that the mission of reconciliation which he had undertaken would not be furthered by opening old sores.[Pg 203]The examples of Austria-Hungary and the connection of Norway with Sweden, cited by him as proofs that a conjunction of two Parliaments worked well, would be generally taken not as encouragements but as warnings. The case of Norway and Sweden has since become a warning indeed. The intricate machinery by which the speaker proposes to regulate the action of his two Parliaments has too much the look of a speculative structure elaborated without reference to the peculiar state of

Ireland and the forces to be encountered there. Of the force of the Catholic priesthood, nothing is said. In fact, the political architect knew little of the country with which he was dealing, having been in it only for three weeks, and then not at a good point of view.

Thus the Irish question, which the greatest among the public men of his time had failed to settle, was once more thrown into the cauldron of party strife.

[Pg 204]

XV

Looking back on these most melancholy annals, we shall find that for their general sadness Nature is as much to be blamed as man. She did well in placing at the side of a country rich in coal and minerals, destined to be manufacturing, one of pasture to supply food. She made a fatal mistake in peopling them with different and uncongenial races. War, in the age of war, and conquest of the weaker by the stronger were sure to be the result. For the form in which conquest came, the Papacy has partly to answer. It used the sword of the Norman adventurer in this case, as it had in the case of England, to crush religious independence and force all churches to bow to its own dominion, while, as the wails of its own partisans in the Becket controversy show, it was itself unworthy of the sovereignty of Christendom. Of this Catholics are bound to take note, as they are of the fact that the Papacy at a later day, by inciting the Irish to rebellion on its own account, brought upon them no small portion of their woes. The Norman [Pg 205]conquest of England had incidentally the bad effect of connecting the English monarchy with dominion in France, and thus turning the forces of the English kings from Ireland, where they might have ended the agony, to a field where they were much worse than wasted. Things could not have taken a more unfortunate course than that of a colony of half-civilized conquerors carrying on war with barbarous tribes of a different race and tongue, yet without force to effect the conquest. The invasion of Edward Bruce, with which England had nothing to do, probably did further harm by breaking up whatever there was of Anglo-Norman order and turning barons into chiefs of Irish Septs. Then the Reformation, a European convulsion involving Ireland, and in the most unfortunate way, since it identified Protestantism with conquest, Catholicism with the struggle for independence, introduced another deadly source of strife, and made Ireland the point of danger to England in her desperate struggle for her own existence and the salvation of the Protestant cause. Otherwise it seems not impossible that the Tudor statesmen, with such a man as Burleigh at their head, might, as they desired, have effected a peaceful settlement. Civilization, not extermination, was their aim. The great[Pg 206] Celtic rebellions of Shane O'Neil, Desmond, and Tyrone, the last two Catholic as well as Celtic, forced upon them the policy of extermination with all its horrors. The rising and massacre of 1641 were the sequel. The vengeance of the victor and the transplantation of the vanquished to Connaught were in their turn the sequel of the rising and massacre of 1641. Of these again the rebound was the Catholic rising of 1688, which, had it been successful, would have ended certainly in the dispossession, probably in the expulsion, possibly in the extermination, of the Protestants. English liberty and religion were at the same time threatened by an Irish Catholic force encamped at Hounslow. The Penal law was execrable; yet hardly more execrable than the Great Act of Attainder. In later days Castle government by corruption was vile; but it was the inevitable accompaniment of the constitution of 1782, the work of Grattan and the Volunteers. Of the master evil of all, the state of the masses of the Irish people, English protectionism must share the blame with the penal laws. But protectionism was then the delusion of the commercial world. Irish patriots were not free from it. To deal with peasant distress was the immediate duty of the Irish Parliament, which[Pg 207] refused even to turn its eyes that way. Peasant distress, organized for rebellion by a revolutionary party at Belfast, itself deriving its inspiration from the American and French revolutions, produced the rising, ever to be accursed and deplored, of 1798.

Irish patriots are apt to talk of England as a single person or, rather, fiend, actuated in her dealings with Ireland by hatred and contempt. England is a nation divided into parties and swayed by varying influences from time to time. The England of Peel and Gladstone is not the England of the Georges, the Stuarts, the Tudors, the Plantagenets, or responsible for the doings of those dynasties. In the evil days of her political history, England, if she oppressed Ireland, also suffered herself. The Liberal party in England did its best for Ireland, and if the Irish members had been what they ought to have been and done what they ought to have done, more rapid progress might have been made. As it was, Ireland shared the great measures of Parliamentary and municipal reform which there had been little prospect of her achieving by herself. She received the boon of national and undenominational education about a generation before

47

England, and but for the reactionary influence of her own[Pg 208] priesthood would have received it in full measure. The same influence maimed as far as it could the undenominational colleges. Nothing could be more deplorable than the long series of coercion acts. But it was hardly to be expected that the English government should strike its flag to assassination and boycotting, or that the British nation would be moved to concession by the inroads of American conspirators combined with domestic rebellion. It was about 1866 that Guizot, talking of Ireland as he walked with an English guest, stopped in his walk and said with an emphatic gesture, "The conduct of England to Ireland for the last thirty years has been admirable." This, before disestablishment, was too strong, as the English guest remarked at the time; but as the judgment of a cool-headed foreign statesman, whose course had not been one of unbroken harmony with England, it was likely to be more just at least to the motives of England than the invectives of O'Connell.

Since the Union there has been no 1641, no 1688, no 1798. The two races and religions have lived generally at peace if not in concord with each other. The religious riots at Belfast are a very mitigated relic of the religious wars of former days. Reform, though its advance has been slow and fitful, has[Pg 209] advanced. Within a generation from the date of the Union, Catholic Emancipation was carried. The tithe-proctor did not very long survive. Presently the State Church itself was abolished. Ireland shared with Great Britain Parliamentary reform, to which the Irish oligarchy could never have consented without political and social convulsion. Not long afterwards came national education, bestowed on Ireland before it was bestowed on England. None of these improvements would directly touch the agrarian sore, the malignity of which was increased by the growth of the Irish population under the reign of order, far beyond the power of the land to maintain it. But relief has been given to famine, and strenuous efforts have been made and are still being made to effect a radical cure. Ireland has enjoyed free trade with Great Britain and with the whole British Empire. Everything has been open to Irish merit and industry. Millions of Irish and their children have found homes in Britain and the colonies. To sever Ireland from Great Britain is still possible. To divide the Irish from the British is not possible. In both islands and in all the colonies the two races are now joined and cannot be put asunder.

Besides, as has already been said, we must always[Pg 210] bear it in mind that we do not see the other side of Destiny's cards. Suppose Ireland had remained the land of the Septs, would her lot certainly have been more happy? Neither at the time of the Norman Conquest nor afterwards do the Septs appear to have shown any tendency to a union such as would have given birth to a national polity and its attendant civilization. For aught we can see, they might have gone on indefinitely, like the clans of the Scottish Highlands, in a state of barbarous strife fatal to progress of every kind. Even their common interest in the struggle against the Anglo-Norman invader produced no general or permanent union. The Brehon law, which was their principal bond, had no executive force and was in itself barbarous, not distinguishing public from private wrong. The Septs warred upon each other not less savagely than the conqueror warred upon them all. If anything like union came at last, it was not political but religious, and brought with it a fatal share in the European war of religions. Nor were conquests other than Anglo-Norman impossible. From the Highlands and islands of Scotland came bodies of marauding adventurers which might have been reënforced, and, in the North at least, have prevailed. It is not certain that without the aid of[Pg 211]John de Bermingham and his Anglo-Normans, the Septs would have got rid of Edward Bruce.

That the interest of Ireland should be regarded as subordinate to that of Great Britain was the principle on which British politicians acted in the days that are past. To the past this principle must now be and indeed has been decisively consigned. That union, to be good for either party, must be good for both, is the accepted basis of discussion. On the other hand, it is not to be assumed that the aspirations of Irish politicians naturally bent on carving out an independent field of action for themselves, are entirely free from the bias of personal ambition or identical with a dispassionate view of the interest of the Irish people. Nor is it to be forgotten that Ulster is a part of Ireland.

There are two questions, perfectly distinct and calling for separate consideration, though they have become blended in the course and for the purposes of the political agitation. One is economical, the other political.

The economical question is whether Ireland can support her present population. Patriotic eloquence will not change her skies, or render it otherwise than cruel to induce her people to stay in a land in which they cannot make their bread.[Pg 212] Instances there may be of barren soil made by the loving industry of the small owner fruitful and capable of supporting a large population; but the industry of the small owner, though it can improve the soil, cannot alter the skies. What is to be desired is a special report, calm and expert, upon this subject. Is Ireland generally capable of being turned with advantage into an arable country? Can wheat or grain of any kind be profitably raised there in face of the competition of the great grain-growing countries such as that now opened, and bidding fair to be opened over a much larger area, in the Canadian Northwest? The small farmer to live must have something to sell. Is there reason to look in any other direction than farming for a speedy extension of Irish industries such as would provide bread sufficient for the population? Is the water-power of Ireland, now that electricity has been developed, likely to do what has been done for England by coal? Is the shipping trade, for which the Irishman has had little opportunity of showing a turn, likely to increase? These are questions which it is for economists, not for politicians or patriotic orators, to decide. It is said that there are tracts of land in Ireland still unoccupied and fit for occupation. If there are, the survey will show the fact. Land[Pg 213] purchase by government subvention is a policy hardly to be pursued unless it is certain that its results will not presently be reversed by nature.

The worst part of emigration is that it carries away the pith and sinews of a nation, taking the strong and leaving the weak, the aged, and unsupported women. It is a pleasant proof, already noticed, of the warmth of the Irish heart that there has been less of solitary and more of family emigration in their case than in those of some other emigrating races. After all, how has the earth been peopled, how have all the nations been formed but by migration?

To turn to the political question. The danger of insurrection has probably passed away. Fenianism has been largely deprived of its trans-Atlantic base, and can no longer look confidently to American sympathy for support and supplies. The Irish vote has less power. Little at least was heard of it in the last presidential election. Yet the political question is still most serious, and presses urgently for settlement; a state of things largely due to the division of parties in the British government which showed its influence in the abandonment of the Crimes Act by the Salisbury administration; in the Maamtrasna debate; and in Mr. Gladstone's[Pg 214]sudden coalition with Parnell; but above all in the votes of British members of the House of Commons for Mr. Gladstone's second Home Rule Bill, giving Ireland a Parliament of her own and representation in the British Parliament at the same time. Parliament still has in it a body of Irish members not only alien but hostile, avowing that their object is not to aid in deliberation but to coerce, playing upon the balance of parties for purposes of their own, degrading the assembly, and distracting the councils of the nation. Nor is the source of this evil confined to the constituencies of Ireland. There is in England and Scotland a large Irish population, which, as was seen in the election of 1885, obeys the voice of the Irish leaders and at their command votes inimically to the country in which it lives and earns its bread. In Ireland itself, moreover, the hell-broth of agitation is kept constantly seething to the inevitable detriment of recuperative effort, which cannot do its full work without security for the future.

As the first step it should be calmly settled what are the specific grievances under which Ireland labours, and which the Imperial legislature cannot, but an Irish Parliament could, remove. Historic wrongs are past remedy. Ireland has more than[Pg 215] her share of representation in Parliament. She has no established Church. If her priesthood would let her, she would have a complete system of national education. Her land law is now far more favourable to the tenant than that of the other kingdoms, and she has been and still is receiving government subventions in aid of the tillers of her soil which English and Scotch tenants do not receive and which would cease if she became independent. Nothing is closed against her people. They have the markets of the whole Empire. All its offices, patronage, and services are perfectly open to them. So long as they will abstain from outrage and murder, they enjoy all the personal privileges of British freemen. It cannot be said that the law has been suspended for any purpose other than the repression of outrage. If the ordinary law and government were very bad, Ulster would hardly have prospered as it has done. If Castle government is the grievance, abolition of it was offered to Ireland long ago and was by her rejected. Let the existing grievances be specified, and let it be seen whether Imperial legislation is incapable of redressing them. The truth is that with the Irish leaders it has not been redress of particular wrongs and grievances or the introduction of practical improvements that has[Pg 216]been the object of desire. Their aim has been to create a nationalist feeling which should end in political separation. Such has been the constant tenor of their appeals to sentiment and the end to which their policy has really pointed.

Suppose Ireland severed from Great Britain, what would be her lot? She would then have to assume all the burdens and responsibilities of an independent nation, including military and naval defence, as well as the entire expense of a separate government. As she could not hope to vie in strength with her powerful neighbour, she would be at that neighbour's mercy; nor, considering the temper in which the parting would take place, would occasions for quarrel be unlikely to arise. Ireland might have to seek the protection and become the vassal of some foreign power. Irish trade would no longer be free of British markets or of the markets of British dependencies. Irish labour would no longer be free of the British labour market. The Indian service and the Imperial services generally would be closed against Irishmen.

49

Nor would Ireland be entirely united in herself or perfectly set free from the hated British influence. She would still have in her the men of Ulster, Saxon and Protestant, antagonistic probably[Pg 217] to the Catholic majority, and if they were pressed in the unequal conflict, stretching out their hands for aid to their fellow-Protestants and kinsmen in Great Britain.

A mere arm of the sea, such as that which divides Ireland from Great Britain, is surely not enough in these days of improved navigation, to form a bar to political union. The distance from London to Dublin is now practically far less than it was a century ago from London to Edinburgh. Nor does there seem any reason why salt water should be fatal. The Ionian Islands are in the kingdom of Greece; so probably some day will be Crete.

If Ireland were detached from Great Britain, into what hands would she fall? The gentry would be extinguished. To excite popular hatred of them as landlords has been the constant aim of the Nationalist leaders. There would be a general repudiation of rent, which the Irish government and judiciary would lack the will, while the British government and judiciary would have lost the power, to prevent. The record of Irish landlordism is not bright. Absenteeism has been a great evil, though the estates of some absentees have been notably well managed. There have been hideously cruel evictions, especially it seems on the lands[Pg 218]purchased by speculators under the Encumbered Estates Act. Landlordism, as mere drawing of rent, is an evil. It is not desirable that any man should own land as a non-resident or own more land than he can manage or superintend. The old feudal law attaching service to lordship of land was sound in principle. But if the Irish gentry would accept that principle, be resident, look after their estates, and do their duty to their tenants, they would probably be accepted by their people as social leaders, and they might play that part with good effect. The life of the French peasant is not the acme either of civilization or of happiness, even though we may make some abatement from the picture presented by Zola in "La Terre." Unhappily the tendency, even in England, seems to be towards the detachment of the owner from his land and the abandonment on his part of every function save that of receiving the rent and spending it, perhaps in some pleasure city or abroad. The decadence of the agricultural interest in England is by some ascribed to this cause.

The gentry being no more, Catholic Ireland would at first fall into the hands of the priesthood. The moral character of the Irish priesthood in the opinion of impartial judges is high, as is that of the priesthood[Pg 219] of French Canada. In both cases ecclesiastical influence is strong, and in both a population virtuous after the Catholic model is the result. The two are probably about the best things that the Roman Catholic Church has to show. But the Roman Catholic religion is mediæval. The training of its ministers inevitably shuts out light which would be fatal to mediæval belief. An Irish peasant lad, having been intellectually secluded for seven years at Maynooth, comes out proof against the intellectual influences and advancing science of his time. He is the mental liegeman and the preacher of the Syllabus, which anathematizes freedom of thought and claims for the Church dominion, not only over the soul but over the body, such as was hers in the Middle Ages. He laid his ban on the Queen's Colleges, and has discouraged and thwarted the extension of popular education. In regard to education and intelligence, he has been in Ireland what he has been in Spain and other countries subject to his sway. In the sphere of industry and commerce the influence has generally been the same. The religious ideal of life with its Church festivals and Saints' Days has prevailed. In Ireland as in Canada the priest inculcates early marriages, the effects of which[Pg 220] may be morally good but are economically perilous. The excessive conversion of the fruits of industry to the unproductive purposes of the Church has already begun to call forth protests.

The power of the Roman Catholic priesthood would be encountered by the stalwart Protestantism of Ulster in the Parliamentary arena as it still is sometimes in the streets of Belfast. It might presently find itself encountered by another adversary, revolutionary Nationalism, the heir of that party of force which broke away from the leadership of O'Connell, the devout son of the Church, and was an object of well-founded suspicion and aversion to the hierarchy of his day. The affinity of this element is to the revolutionary party in other countries; and if, like the United Irishmen of Belfast, it has been willing to act with allies devoted to the Church, it is not itself devout, as the Church, if she comes to share power with it, may be led to feel.

The idea of unity of race as a basis of Irish nationality has little support. In the North there is a strong and masterful Saxon element. There must be a large Anglo-Saxon and English element in the old Pale. The men of Tipperary, though characteristically Irish, are believed to be descendants of Cromwellians. There is Huguenot blood.

[Pg 221]The revival of Erse as a national language is surely a patriotic dream. How is it possible to revive a language all but dead, with no valuable literature or wealth of printed books, in face of a language which has a grand literature, is spoken by all the educated classes, indeed almost universally, in Ireland, and is necessary for intercourse with Great Britain. O'Connell, we are told, had no great sympathy with the revival of Irish archæology, and no sympathy at all with the project of reviving the Irish language. He recognized the superior utility of the English tongue as the medium of all modern communication, and saw without regret the gradual disuse of Erse. Fancy and sentiment may prevail among a literary class which nevertheless will hardly carry its patriotism so far as to darken its own mind by unlearning English.

"Ireland ought to be governed in accordance with Irish ideas." Such is the current saying, and it sounds wise. But statesmanship would hardly act upon it before taking measures to learn what ideas are peculiarly Irish and whether they are features of national character, innate and indelible, and not traces of historic accident or fancies instilled in the course of political agitation. The perpetuation of weaknesses accidentally contracted cannot[Pg 222] be wise for man or nation. The political idea which seems most characteristic is the tendency to personal leadership rather than to self-government or constitutional rule. But this has been common to all races in early times. It was fostered and prolonged by the circumstances of Irish history. It could hardly be pronounced incapable of modification by familiarity with free institutions.

What would be the political constitution of an independent Ireland? How would its form be settled? The political training of the people generally since they came out of political thraldom has been agitation against government and law; their only notion of rule has been personal. Nor is a hierarchy friendly to political liberty. To set up a stable democracy in Ireland, if that is the aim of the revolutionary party, would surely be an arduous undertaking.

All who look coolly into the matter apart from faction and its necessities have pronounced that the choice lies between separation and legislative union. Two Parliaments, two nations; so all wisdom says and so experience before the Union proved. The forces which under Grattan's constitution held the two Parliaments together in strained and precarious fellowship, the nomination boroughs, the[Pg 223] pension list, the sinecures, the peerages, the bishoprics, would no longer exist. What is even more important, there would no longer be an oligarchical and exclusionist Parliament in Ireland dependent on British support for its ascendency, perhaps even for the security of its lands. Antagonism would almost inevitably ensue; the more surely as the partners would set out with the embitterment of a divorce. Nothing apparently could avert collision; the result of which would be repression, making the latter end worse than the first.

The proposal of federation is surely preposterous. It would be necessary first to cut the United Kingdom in two and create an Irish government in order that negotiations for a federal union might be set on foot. But how could there be a federation of two states, one of them enormously superior in power to the other? What sort of deliberative assembly would the federal council be?

Another plan is to form a federation of the four nationalities, as they are assumed to be, England, Scotland, Ireland, and Wales; wrenching apart the members of a great nation which have long been united and cancelling the highest work of British statesmanship. Here again federation could not work. England being so much the predominant[Pg 224] partner, the result would almost certainly be a perpetual league of the three minor powers against her domination. The federal system is applicable only to a group of tolerably equal States. The restoration of the Heptarchy with the addition of Scotland, divided into Highland and Lowland, and the four provinces of Ireland erected into States, would be a comparatively practicable system. The present condition of the Federal system in the United States does not encourage experiments of that kind.

The mildest proposal of all is devolution; in other words, the concession to Ireland of a larger measure of local self-government. This probably would be readily granted to any extent compatible with supremacy of law and security of life and property, which no government without abdicating its plainest duty can forgo. Gradual extension of local self-government would not entail any acute crisis or bring on any party conflict. The Lord-lieutenancy, Parliament has already shown itself ready to abolish. It was in deference to the wish of Ireland that it has been retained. The only thing in the way of undue centralization of which, so far as the writer remembers, his Irish friends complained, was the necessity of carrying Irish causes to Westminster as the final[Pg 225] court of appeal. Whether concession on this point would be feasible it is for legal authorities to say.

However, it can hardly be doubted that in the course of this struggle a sentiment has been cultivated among the people of Ireland for which it is wise as well as kind in some way to provide satisfaction. The Irishman being of lively sensibility and impressible through sight has never seen the power which really governs him. A session or two of the Imperial Parliament held at Dublin for the settlement of Irish questions would probably have had a very good effect, but it was thought to entail too much inconvenience. Would there be any objection to empowering the Irish members of both Houses to sit annually at Dublin as a preparatory House of Irish legislation framing bills to be commended to Parliament? There would then be something in College Green. The experiment would involve none of the difficulties or perils of a statutory division of the powers of Parliament. It would be at first on the footing of an experiment, nor would it preclude further concessions if further concessions should be found needful.

With the question of national character, social or industrial, and its special requirements, I do not pretend to deal. It has been treated systematically,[Pg 226] perhaps for the first time, by an excellent authority, Sir Horace Curzon Plunkett, in his "Ireland in the New Century." Of Irish character a part may be aboriginal and fundamental. A part probably is the result of historical accident more or less ingrained, and probably capable of modification. I am told that Irish character has been even acquiring a more serious cast since I watched the Tipperary steeplechases or stood on the fair-ground of Ballinasloe. Not a little, so far as the masses are concerned, is probably the work of a priesthood strongly and inherently reactionary, which has exercised the same influence on the ideal of life, character, mind, and industry here as in other Catholic countries. Ireland is perhaps happy in having been cut off from the prodigious development of luxury and dissipation which, as social writers tell us, has been taking place on the other side of the Channel as well as from the domination of the stock-exchange. She may in this way become a saving element in the social character of the United Kingdom.

Is it vain to hope that for the settlement of a question so vital party may for one short hour suspend its war? What far-off object of aggrandizement can be half so important as a contented and loyal Ireland.

[Pg 227]

AN ACCOUNT OF THE IRISH LAND CODE
By Hugh J. McCann, B.L.

The Irish landlord, poor as his circumstances were before the famine, was in many instances reduced to sorer straits after the terrible scourge had passed away. The good landlord, anxious to do his duty by his tenants, helped them as far as his mortgages and other financial burdens would allow. The tyrannical one, regardless of the sufferings of his victims, sought to extract impossible rents from an unfortunate tenantry who had scarcely the means of subsistence. The Encumbered Estates Act, it was thought, would relieve the tension. It empowered a court specially constituted for the purpose to order the sale of estates encumbered with debt, on the petition of any person sufficiently interested as owner or creditor.

Landlordism, it was thought, would, by this act, be relieved of much that made it tyrannical, even when it meant well. But the act was a failure. It was worse. It was the means of wrecking many[Pg 228] a fortune, and driving many a proprietor to ruin. Men who, in hard times, were doing well for their tenants and their country under difficult circumstances were driven from the land.

The act came into operation towards the end of 1849. A wild rush was made by creditors to the court. Prices fell with amazing rapidity, and landed property became a drug in the market. Valuable properties failed to realize sufficient to meet the mortgages, and their owners were inevitably ruined.

A new class of landlord now appeared on the scene in the person of the speculator, who bought up the bankrupt properties as they presented themselves. The new proprietors had nothing in common with their tenantry. They knew little of their needs and requirements and cared less. They had but one interest and that was a commercial one. To make their properties realize a good dividend on their outlay was their one concern, and up went the rents accordingly. Such was the fate of the unfortunate tenants who were allowed to continue as tenants of the new proprietor. This was bad enough, but those that were given notice to quit were even more cruelly wronged. Compensation for wrongful disturbance was not [Pg 229]recognized in Ireland in 1850, and tenant property amounting to three millions sterling was sold to pay the landlord's creditors.

Nothing could demonstrate more clearly how utterly rotten was the whole land system in Ireland at the time. Landlord and tenant alike were in a miserable plight. Rents fell heavily in arrear, and evictions were the order of the day. The landlord played the bold game, struck hard, and without mercy. The tenant sought protection in combination and conspiracy. Such was the condition of Ireland when thoughtful men sought by legislation to cure the crying evils of the time. Many remedies were proposed between 1850 and 1860, but none of them reached the stage of legislative enactment. In the latter year, however, Cardwell made an attempt to place the law of landlord and tenant on a better footing.

In spite of a good deal of opposition, government succeeded in placing two important measures on the Statute Book, viz.: the Landed Property (Ireland) Improvement Act, 1860, and the Landlord and Tenant Law Amendment Act (Ireland) of the same year. By the former limited owners were enabled, subject to judicial sanction, to charge the inheritance with the cost of specified improvements,[Pg 230] and to bind their successors for stated periods. Agricultural leases for a period of twenty-one years or less could be given by the limited owners without judicial intervention, but every improvement lease required the sanction of the chairman of the county in which the lands were situated.

To tenants the right of compensation was granted for certain specified improvements made by them, provided that before entering on the improvements they made them the subject of an agreement with the landlord, or had given notice of his intention to improve, and the landlord had not notified his objection within a period of three months from receipt of the notice. The principle of retrospective compensation was not, as yet, admitted.

The second act consolidated the existing law of landlord and tenant, and made some important changes in procedure.

The relationship of landlord and tenant, hitherto based on *tenure*, as in England, was henceforth to be founded on *contract*.

Before proceeding to examine its provisions, it might be well to point out that the common law rights of Irish agricultural tenants were in the absence of special customs governed since the reign of James I. by English common law rules. The[Pg 231] English system of land tenure was imposed upon the country by virtue of conquest. But the circumstances of the two countries were entirely different.

In England the landlord owned the soil and everything on it. The dwelling houses and out-offices, the farm roads, the drainage, were built by him or his predecessors. He let a holding to a tenant as a going concern, and for the holding so equipped he received rent. The relations between landlord and tenant in England rested on a business footing. If the tenant did not feel satisfied with his farm or his lot, he moved on. There were none of the ties there, either of attachment or of interest, that existed in Ireland. In Ireland the tenant or his predecessor provided, by his labours or his savings, the whole equipment of the farm. His family for generations back occupied the same plot, and he dearly learned to know and love every stone and hedge about the place. In England the improvements were effected by the landlord out of the rent paid him by the tenant, and, of course, were legally his by the law of the land. In Ireland the improvements, almost universally made by the tenant, became at common law the property of the landlord, who was under no *legal* obligation to compensate the tenant for them on ejecting him from his [Pg 232]holding. The following extract from the report of the Devon Commission contrasts the practice in the two countries very well. "The Commission finds on all hands, it is admitted, that, according to the general practice in Ireland, the landlord builds neither dwelling-house nor farm-offices, nor puts fences, gates, etc., into good order before he lets his land to a tenant. The cases in which a landlord does any of those things are the exceptions. The system, however, of giving aid in these matters is becoming more prevalent. In most cases whatever is done in the way of building is done by the tenant, and in the ordinary language of the country dwelling-houses, farm-buildings, and even the making of the fences are described by the general word 'improvements,' which is thus employed to denote the necessary adjuncts to a farm, without which in England or Scotland no tenant would be found to rent it."

What I have said represents the general, but, I should add, not the universal, condition of things in Ireland at this time.

In parts of the country, especially in Ulster, certain customs prevailed which recognized that a tenant was something more than a rent producer. They denied the right of the landlord to raise rents[Pg 233] by reason of any value added to the soil by the tenant's outlay. They recognized a right of continuous occupancy by the tenant at a fair rent. This right, called tenant right, became on some properties of immense value, and was often sold by an out-going tenant at a price exceeding in value the fee simple purchase of the holding. In Ulster more than anywhere else in Ireland the custom was very widely prevalent, but was as yet without the sanction of the law.

But I have digressed from the Act of 1860. In dealing with the Act of 1870, what I have just said will be of importance. The Landlord and Tenant Act, 1860, otherwise known as "Deasy's Act," is a voluminous measure of one hundred and five sections which may be conveniently grouped into three sections. The first deals with the *Contract of Tenancy*, the second with *Surrenders and Assignments*, and the third with the *Methods of Procedure*. Section three enacts that "the relation of landlord and tenant shall be deemed to be founded on the express or implied contract of the parties." The conduct of the parties may imply a contract of tenancy, payment of rent being evidence, but not irrefutable evidence, of its existence.

Section four requires that "every lease or [Pg 234]contract, with respect to lands whereby the relations of landlord and tenant is intended to be created for any freehold estate or interest, or for any definite period of time, not being from year to year, or any lesser period, shall be by *deed* executed, or *note in writing* signed by the landlord or his agent." It is further provided that a tenant may, if there be no agreement to the contrary, remove his fixtures within two months of its determination by an uncertain event. Two covenants are implied in the contract of tenancy by each of the parties thereto. The landlord by his lease implies an agreement on the part of himself and his successors that he has a good title to make it, and that the tenant shall have quiet and peaceable enjoyment of his holding.

The tenant agrees to pay rent, taxes, and impositions payable by the tenant, and to keep the premises in good and substantial repair and condition; and, secondly, to give up peaceable possession of the demised premises in good and substantial repair and condition on the determination of the lease, subject to any right of removal or of compensation for improvements that may have lawfully arisen in respect of them, and to any right of surrender in case of the destruction of the subject-matter of the contract.

[Pg 235]*Surrenders and Assignments* may be made (1) by deed, (2) by a note in writing, or (3) by operation of law.

Sections forty-five to one hundred and two deal with actions for the recovery of rent and actions of ejectment. The most important provision is that which provides that if a tenant has had a decree given against him in an action of ejectment, he may be restored to his holding on applying to the court within six months, and paying the rent with arrears and costs.

Such are the main features of Deasy's Act. Beyond consolidating and regularizing the existing law it achieved nothing. A decided advance, however, was made in the Landlord and Tenant (Ireland) Act, 1870, which was restricted in its operation to agricultural and pastoral tenancies. We have seen how there existed in Ulster and other parts of the country certain customs favourable to the tenant. To the Ulster custom, as it was called, Ulster was indebted for exceptional prosperity.

The contentment of its agricultural population was in strange contrast to the seething discontent of the other parts of the country. Much of the thrift and plenty that exists in parts of Ulster to-day can be traced back to the exceptional treatment[Pg 236] accorded to the tenants of Ulster long before legislation came to the aid of their less fortunate brethren south of the Boyne. The aim of the Land Act of 1870 was to place the latter class in a similar position to the Northerns. The act legalized the Ulster custom and similar usages. It gave tenants not subject to these a right to be compensated for their improvements on quitting their holdings, and guaranteed a measure of security by providing compensation for disturbance. What is "disturbance" is a question for the court, and must be decided on the facts of each particular case.

Agreements not to improve the holding, or not to claim for improvements, are declared void. If the holding be subject to the Ulster custom, there is a general presumption that the improvements belong to the tenant.

The term "improvements" shall mean in relation to a holding (1) any work which, being executed, adds to the letting value of the holding, on which it is executed and is suitable to such holding; and (2) tillages, manures, or other like farming works, the benefit of which is unexhausted at the time of the tenant quitting his holding.

We have not proceeded far before it becomes apparent that to secure to the tenant the full [Pg 237]enjoyment of his own property was the line along which land legislation was travelling. The Act of 1870 went some distance in this direction. But the great advance was not made till ten years after, when Gladstone proposed to establish a tribunal which would assess and fix the property of the two partners in the dual ownership of land in Ireland. The act recognized and legalized dual ownership. It created a partnership between two parties whose interests were hostile. It was a great act, and did incalculable good, but many years were not to elapse until it became evident that a return to single ownership—but this time by the tenant—was absolutely necessary. The endeavours to work dual ownership irretrievably broke down.

Both parties had little confidence in the Land Court established by the Act of 1881.

The landlord complained that his property was being confiscated; the tenant believed that he was still paying rent on his own improvements. The act was meant to give tenants fixity of tenure, fair rent, and free sale. A new judicial body, the Irish Land Commission, with jurisdiction to hear and determine all matters of law or fact arising under the act, was established. The commission consists of three commissioners—one a judicial [Pg 238]commissioner and numerous assistant commissioners appointed by the lord lieutenant for the time being with the approval of the treasury. This is not the place to examine the provisions of this complicated measure minutely, but as it is the foundation of much of the land legislation that followed, it is important that its main provisions be understood.

The act distinguishes between "present" tenancies and "future" tenancies, a "present" tenancy being "a tenancy subsisting at the time of the passing of the act, or created before the first day of January, 1883, in a holding in which a tenancy was subsisting at the time of the passing of the act, and every tenancy to which the act applies shall be deemed to be a present tenancy until the contrary is proved."

A "future" tenancy means a tenancy beginning after the passing of the act. The act applies only to agricultural and pastoral holdings. It gives qualified powers to both "present" and "future" tenants to dispose of their holdings for the best price they can get, or to mortgage them if they think fit.

Fixity of tenure was secured by enabling a tenant to convert his interest into what is called in the act a *statutory term*. Such a term may be created by[Pg 239] an agreement between the landlord and tenant for an increased rent, or by having a fair rent fixed, or by filing in court an agreement for a judicial rent. A *statutory term* can be created only in respect of a "present" tenancy except when in regard to a "future" tenancy the tenant has agreed with the landlord to an increased rent. The provisions as to the fixing of a fair rent apply only to "present" tenancies. Section three of the act gives a tenant power to dispose of his holding by bequest. Perhaps the most important provisions of the act are those enabling a landlord or tenant to have a "fair rent" fixed.

Either party may apply to the court to have the rent made a *judicial rent*. The court fixes this rent after considering all the circumstances of the case, holding, and district, and having regard to the interests of both parties. No rent shall be payable in respect of improvements made by the tenant unless he has been already compensated for them by the landlord. In the administration of the act the word "improvements" has given rise to endless litigation. In the now famous case of Adams *v.* Dunseath it was held that "improvements" meant improvement works and not increased letting value. It was also held in a case affecting the same holding[Pg 240]that a tenant is entitled to "a fair return by way of annual allowance in respect of the present capital value of his improvement works which may be estimated by way of percentage on such capital value; and if after making this percentage there is still a surplus of increased letting value, it is within the exclusive jurisdiction of the Land Commission to determine whether, and in what proportions, such surplus shall be divided between landlord and tenant." It was further laid down that the Land Commission was to treat "the latent and dormant resources of the soil, as let by the landlord to the tenant, as the property of the landlord, and the development of those resources by the tenant as the act of the tenant."

This act was undoubtedly a great charter for the tenants and created something like a revolution in Ireland. It contained many defects, and was marred by many blemishes, but on the whole it was a masterly attempt to settle the question. Like much of the land legislation for Ireland, most of its shortcomings were due to a reckless disregard on the part of British ministers for Irish opinion. Indeed, this was the cause of most of the amending legislation that followed.

Under the Act of 1881 "fair rents" were fixed for[Pg 241] periods of fifteen years, when they were again ripe for revision. Roughly speaking, the old non-judicial rents were reduced by twenty per cent on an average to convert them into first term rents. These again were further reduced by twenty per cent on an average for the second term. This, of course, played havoc with the landlord's income, and did not materially benefit the tenant, the prices of the produce of whose farm was falling with even greater rapidity. The experiment of dual ownership had been tried and was found wanting; a return to single ownership was sought for by the series of acts known as the Land Purchase Acts.

It was not till 1885 that the experiment of land purchase was seriously tried in Ireland, but it is right to say that the question first came before the public in a practical form so far back as 1869 in the discussions on the disestablishment of the Irish Episcopal Church. At that time Mr. Bright proposed to increase the number of owners of land in Ireland by allowing the glebe tenants to purchase the property attached to the glebes. The idea was embodied in the Irish Church Act, and over six thousand occupying owners were thus created. Under this act three-fourths of the purchase money was advanced by the State, and the balance paid in cash[Pg 242] by the purchasers. The money was advanced by the State for thirty-two years, the shortest period allowed by any of the acts. From the tenant's point of view this act cannot be said to have been an unqualified success. The price of land was high at the time, and the purchasers having bought high sustained the whole burden of the sudden fall in the prices of produce which almost immediately succeeded the conclusion of their bargains. In 1870 and in 1881 there were embodied in the acts of these years provisions to enable tenants to purchase their holdings; but the procedure to be followed was made so complicated that the tenants did not avail themselves of the purchase clauses to any great extent. The insignificant number of sixteen hundred sales were completed under the two acts.

In 1885 a Conservative government came into power, and though their term of office was of short duration, they introduced and passed a measure which, by its marvellous and, I might add, its unexpected success, pointed the direction and paved the way for all future legislation for the settlement of the land problem in Ireland. Back to single ownership was the keynote of the measure. Hitherto the credit or discredit of all legislation on the land problem belonged to the Liberals. They strove to[Pg 243] make dual ownership a possibility. Conservative statesmen sought for a settlement in the opposite direction.

In sales under all the purchase acts from 1885 to the Act of 1903 all the purchase money is advanced by the State to the selling landlord, and is charged by the State to the tenant who purchases. The tenant repays the amount borrowed or "advanced," to use the language of the acts, in annual instalments, which instalments clear off not only the original "advance," but the accumulated interest.

Roughly speaking, the procedure is this. The landlord and tenant, having agreed on a price, sign an agreement for sale, and file it with the Land Commission, which body has the carriage, so to speak, of all purchase transactions, as well as all other transactions under the land acts. The holding is inspected by the Land Commission which, having been satisfied that the land in question is security for the "advance," pay the purchase money to the landlord and collect from the tenant the annual instalments necessary to repay it to the State.

The plan of the Act of 1885, better known as the Ashbourne Act from the fact that it was Lord Ashbourne who introduced the measure to the lords, was simple in the extreme, and to this is due, in no[Pg 244] small measure, its rapid success. It was easily understood by the people, and so popular did it become that in three years the money provided by it was completely exhausted.

In 1888 a second bill was passed under which an additional sum of five millions—this was the amount provided by the Ashbourne Act—was set aside for purchase. Under the two measures 25,368 owners were created.

"Almost from the start," writes Mr. George Fottrell (a gentleman well qualified to discuss the question of land purchase in Ireland) in the *Morning Post*, "the Ashbourne Act was a success. During the first five years of its working, the 'advances' actually paid over by the Land Commission to landlords amounted annually on an average to £1,250,000 sterling. The 'applications' represented a considerably larger sum. By 1887 they had more than exhausted the £5,000,000 which had been voted by Parliament for the Ashbourne Act, in 1885, and thereon a further sum of £5,000,000 was voted. The scheme continued to work well; the 'applications' came in steadily but with no feverish haste, the largest total sum applied for under the Ashbourne Act in any one year being in 1887 when it reached £3,700,000.[Pg 245] In each of the next two years it reached just two millions. In 1890 it had dropped to less than a million and a half; in 1891 it was slightly in excess of that amount. By 1891 it was plain that the second vote of five millions had been virtually absorbed, and that Parliament must be applied to for further money. To cool-headed people in Ireland it seemed that the obvious course was to ask for a small grant, say of ten millions, so as to continue to test cautiously the usefulness of an act which had so far worked well, while by the very smallness of the grant keeping in reserve a check on the expansion of the act if it should prove to work mischievously.

"This course was not taken. In 1891 Parliament was asked to make a much larger grant. Over thirty millions were voted, but coupled with conditions which made the money useless."

Mr. Balfour's act, the Purchase Act of 1891, was extremely complicated. Under it Ireland was entitled to draw upon Imperial credit to the extent of £33,000,000. The rate of interest payable by the purchasers was substantially the same as under the acts of 1885 and 1888, the period of repayment in the three cases being forty-nine years.

But a change was made in the method of payment[Pg 246] to the landlord. Previous to 1891, he had been always paid in cash. Under the Balfour Act he was paid in guaranteed land stock. There were many complicated provisions in regard to the creation of a guarantee fund, an insurance fund, and other safeguards. The complexity of the measure and the procedure under it, and the consequent delays in completing any transactions in a reasonable time, acted as a deterrent to intending purchasers and the act was virtually a failure. At this point it is well, perhaps, to summarize the results of the working of land purchase under the acts already dealt with. We have seen that a total sum of (say) £44,000,000 was made available by the various acts for land purchase. Out of this a total sum of £21,182,268 has been expended, leaving about twenty-three millions still available. Under all the acts up to and including that of 1891, 62,241 tenants purchased their holdings, 6057 under the Church Act, 877 under the Land Act of 1870, 731 under the Act of 1881, 25,368 under the Purchase Acts of 1885 and 1888, and the balance of about 30,000 became purchasers by means of the Act of 1891.

Numerous and extensive as these operations were, it is satisfactory to note, and it redounds to the credit of the Irish people, that Mr. Wyndham,[Pg 247] when introducing his Land Bill of 1902, was able to assure the House of Commons that Irish Land Purchase had this one merit that the State had incurred no loss under it and was exposed to no risk. In no case did an Irish tenant break his bargain. There was no case of bad debt to mention.

One of the first stumbling-blocks to a tenant proposing to purchase under the Act of 1891 was that he was unable to know, or even approximately gauge, what was the actual sum he would have to pay, by way of annuity, each year. This was a serious flaw, and helped more than anything else perhaps to clog the wheels of purchase. This state of things, however, was remedied by the Purchase Act of 1896, by which the maximum sum payable in any year was an instalment at the rate of £4 per cent on the purchase money, no matter at what number of years' purchase of his rent the tenant might buy. Most of the cumbrous restrictions of the Act of 1891 were removed, and once more the applications began to tumble in. In 1895-1896 the applications received numbered less than half a million. In 1897-1898 and in 1898-1899 they reached nearly two millions. A steady decrease then set in, but on the whole purchase proceeded at a satisfactory pace.

[Pg 248]A strange condition of things now existed in Ireland, and a condition of things that could not last. Here and there over the country there existed a contented peasantry, the virtual owners of their holdings, paying a reasonable annuity for a definite period to the State. If they had not the sense of complete ownership, they had the very next best thing to it. They knew that if they themselves were not the absolute owners of their holdings during their lives, their children and their children's children would be, and they set to work with a heart and a will to work and improve their farms, knowing full well that the results of their labour would, at last, be theirs, and could not be wrung from them by the whims or exigencies of the landlord. On the other side of the fence, or river, the tenant who had not purchased or, perhaps, could not purchase, for his landlord would not sell, continued to pay a rent sometimes exorbitant, but always higher than his friend the purchaser close by. Such was the position of the tenant's side of the question. Now let us examine the landlord's.

Under the Act of 1896 the landlord was paid in government stock. Between the years 1891 and 1896 government stock rose from 96 to 110. A premium of ten per cent was a strong incentive to[Pg 249] the landlord to sell. If he had an estate worth £5000, he received in reality for it £5500, for he was credited with £5000 stock which, sold on change, realized £5500 in cash. In some cases, where the estate was mortgaged, the gain was even more. This was gold finding for the landlord until the price of stock fell, which it did and with a vengeance. Stock which in 1897 stood at 113 fell in 1901 to 91. The fall again clogged the wheels, and the question once again became the burning question of the hour. It is right to say here that there were other forces at work which made the landlord anxious to get out, if he could at all, on reasonable terms. The fall in the price of produce continued, and the Land Commission, which had under the Act of 1881 twice revised the rentals, and reduced them each time by twenty per cent on an average, were preparing for the third revision. The landlords looked forward to 1911 with fear and trembling. With their estates mostly heavily mortgaged, and the third revision at hand, they were as anxious as the tenants, if not more so, that Parliament should step in to their mutual aid. It did so in the Land Act of 1903. The introduction of this measure was preceded by a conference of landlords and tenants, representatives in Ireland which met in the Mansion[Pg 250] House, Dublin, and after five sittings reported as follows:—

"Whereas it is expedient that the land question in Ireland be settled so far as it is practicable and without delay,

"And whereas the existing position of the land question is adverse to the improvement of the soil of Ireland, leads to unending controversies and law-suits between owners and occupiers, retards progress in the country, and constitutes a grave danger to the state,

"And whereas an opportunity of settling once for all the differences between owners and occupiers in Ireland is very desirable,

"And whereas such settlement can only be effected upon a basis mutually satisfactory to the owners and occupiers of the land,

"And whereas certain representatives of owners and occupiers have been desirous of endeavouring to find such basis, and for that purpose have met in conference together,

"And whereas certain particulars of agreement have been formulated, discussed, and passed at the conference, and it is desirable that the same should be put into writing and submitted to his Majesty's government,

[Pg 251]"After consideration and discussion of various schemes submitted to the conference, we are agreed:—

"1. That the only satisfactory settlement of the land question is to be effected by the substitution of an occupying proprietary in lieu of the existing system of dual ownership.

"2. That the process of direct interference by the State in purchase and resale is in general tedious and unsatisfactory; and that, therefore, except in cases where at least half the occupiers or the owners so desire, and except in districts included in the operations of the congested districts board, the settlement should be made between owner and occupier, subject to the necessary investigation by the State as to title, rental, and security.

"3. That it is desirable in the interests of Ireland that the present owners of land should not as a result of any settlement be expatriated, or, having received payment for their land, should find no object for remaining in Ireland, and that as the effect of a far-reaching settlement must necessarily be to cause the sale of tenancies throughout the whole of Ireland, inducements should, wherever practicable, be afforded to selling owners to continue to reside in that country.

[Pg 252]"4. That for the purpose of obtaining such a result, an equitable price ought to be paid to the owners, which should be based upon income.

"Income, as it appears to us, is second term rents—including all rents fixed subsequent to the passing of the Act of 1896—or their fair equivalent.

"5. That the purchase price should be based upon income as indicated above, and should be either the assurance by the State of such income, or the payment of a capital sum producing such income at three per cent or at three and one-fourth per cent, if guaranteed by the State, or if the existing powers of trustees be sufficiently enlarged.

"Costs of collection where such exist, not exceeding ten per cent, are not included for the purpose of these paragraphs in the word 'income.'

"6. That such income or capital sum should be obtainable by the owners:—

"(*a*) Without the requirement of capital outlay upon their part, such as would be involved by charges for proving title to sell. Six years' possession, as proposed in the bill brought forward in the session of 1902, appears to us a satisfactory method of dealing with the matter.

"(*b*) Without the requirement of outlay to prove title to receive the purchase money.

[Pg 253]"(*c*) Without unreasonable delay.

"(*d*) Without loss of income pending reinvestment.

"(*e*) And without leaving a portion of the capital sum as a guarantee deposit.

"7. That, as a necessary inducement to selling owners to continue to reside in Ireland, the provision of the bill introduced by the chief secretary for Ireland in the session of 1902 with regard to the purchase of mansion houses, demesne lands, and home farms by the State, and resale by it to the owners, ought to be extended.

"8. We suggest that in certain cases it would be to the advantage of the State as insuring more adequate security, and also an advantage to owners in such cases, if upon the purchase by the State of the mansion house and demesne land and resale to the owner, the house and demesne land should not be considered a security to the mortgages.

"9. That owners wishing to sell portions of grazing land in their own hands for the purpose of enlarging neighbouring tenancies should be entitled to make an agreement with the tenants, and that in the event of proposed purchase by the tenants such grazing land may be considered as part of the tenancies for the purpose of purchase.

[Pg 254]"10. That, in addition to the income, or capital sum producing the income, the sum due for rent from the last rent day till the date of the agreement for purchase and the hanging gale should be paid by the State to the owner.

"11. That all liabilities by the owner which run with the land, such as head-rents, quit-rents, and tithe-rent charge, should be redeemed, and the capital sum paid for such redemption deducted from the purchase money payable to the owner. Provided always that the price of redemption should be calculated on a basis not higher, as regards annual value, than is used in calculating the purchase price of the estate. In any special cases where it may have to be calculated upon a different basis, the owner should not suffer thereby. Owners liable to drainage charges should be entitled to redeem same upon equitable terms, having regard to the varying rates of interest at which such loans were made.

"12. That the amount of the purchase money payable by the tenants should be extended over a series of years, and be at such a rate, in respect of principal and interest, as will at once secure a reduction of not less than fifteen per cent, or more than twenty-five per cent on second term rents or[Pg 255] their fair equivalent, with further periodical reductions as under existing land purchase acts until such time as the treasury is satisfied that the loan has been repaid. This may involve some assistance from the State beyond the use of its credit, which, under circumstances hereinafter mentioned, we consider may reasonably be granted. Facilities should be provided for the redemption at any time of the purchase money or part thereof by payment of the capital or any part thereof.

"13. That the hanging gale, where such custom exists, should be included in the loan and paid off in the instalments to be paid by the purchasing occupier, and should not be a debt immediately recoverable from the occupier, but the amount of rent ordinarily payable for the period between the date when the last payment fell due and the date of agreement for sale should be payable as part of the first instalment.

"14. That counties wholly or partly under the operations of the congested districts board, or other districts of a similar character (as defined by the Congested Districts Board Acts and by section four, clause one, of Mr. Wyndham's Land Purchase Amendment Bill of last session), will require separate and exceptional treatment with a view to the better[Pg 256] distribution of the population and of the land, as well as for the acceleration and extension of these projects for migration and enlargement of holdings which the congested districts board, as at present constituted and with its limited powers, has hitherto found it impossible to carry out upon an adequate scale.

"15. That any project for the solution of the Irish Land Question should be accompanied by a settlement of the evicted tenants' question upon an equitable basis.

"16. That sporting and riparian rights should remain as they are, subject to any provisions of existing Land Purchase Acts.

"17. That the failure to enforce the Labourers Acts in certain portions of the country constitutes a serious grievance, and that in districts where, in the opinion of the local government board, sufficient accommodation has not been made for the housing of the labouring classes, power should be given to the local government board, in conjunction with the local authorities, to acquire sites for houses and allotments.

"18. That the principle of restriction upon subletting might be extended to such control as may be practicable over resales of purchasers' interest and[Pg 257] mortgages, with a view to maintaining unimpaired the value of the State's security for outstanding instalments on loans.

"And whereas we are agreed that no settlement can give peace and contentment to Ireland or afford reasonable and fair opportunity for the development of the resources of the country, which fails to satisfy the just claims of both owners and occupiers,

"And whereas such settlement can only be effected by the assistance of the State, which, as a principle, has been employed in former years,

"And whereas it appears to us that, for the healing of differences and the welfare of the country, such assistance should be given, and can be given, and can effect a settlement without either undue cost to the treasury or appreciable risk with regard to the money advanced, we are of opinion that any reasonable difference arising between the sum advanced by the State, and ultimately repaid to it, may be justified by the following considerations:—

"That for the future welfare of Ireland, and for the smooth working of any measure dealing with the transfer of land, it is necessary:—

"1. That the occupiers should be started on their new career as owners on a fair and favourable basis, insuring reasonable chances of success, and[Pg 258] that in view of the responsibilities to be assumed by them they should receive some inducement to purchase.

"2. That the owners should receive some recognition of the facts that selling may involve sacrifice of sentiment, that they have already suffered heavily by the operation of the land acts, and that they should receive some inducement to sell.

"3. That for the benefit of the whole community it is of the greatest importance that income derived from sale of property in Ireland should continue to be expended in Ireland.

"And we further submit that, as a legitimate setoff against any demand upon the State, it must be borne in mind that, upon the settlement of the land question in Ireland, the cost of administration of the law and the cost of the Royal Irish Constabulary would be materially and permanently lessened.

"We do not, at the present time, desire to offer further recommendations upon the subject of finance which must necessarily be regulated by the approval of the government to the principles of the proposals above formulated except that, in our opinion, the principles of reduction of the sinking fund in the event of loss to the State by an increase of the value[Pg 259] of money should be extended by the inclusion of the principle of increase of the sinking fund in favour of the purchasers in the event of gain to the State by decrease in the value of money.

"Inasmuch as one of the main conditions of success in reference to any land purchase scheme must be its prompt application and the avoidance of those complicated investigations and legal delays which have hitherto clogged all legislative proposals for settling the relations between Irish landlords and tenants, we deem it of urgent importance that no protracted period of time should ensue before a settlement based upon the above-mentioned principles is carried out; that the executive machinery should be effective, competent, and speedy, and that investigations conducted by it should not entail cost upon owner or occupier; and, as a further inducement to despatch, we suggest that any state aid, apart from loans which may be required for carrying out a scheme of land purchase as herein proposed, should be limited to transactions initiated within five years after the passing of the act.

"We wish to place on record our belief that an unexampled opportunity is at the present moment afforded his Majesty's government of effecting a reconciliation of classes in Ireland upon terms[Pg 260] which, as we believe, involve no permanent increase of Imperial expenditure in Ireland; and that there would be found on all sides an earnest desire to coöperate with the government in securing the success of a Land Purchase Bill, which, by effectively and rapidly carrying out the principles above indicated, would bring peace and prosperity to the country.

"Signed at the Mansion House, Dublin, this third day of January, 1903.

"DUNRAVEN (*Chairman*)	JOHN REDMOND
"MAYO	WM. O'BRIEN
"W. H. HUTCHESON POE	T. W. RUSSELL
"NUGENT T. EVERARD	T. C. HARRINGTON"

It soon transpired that the idea of a conference between landlords' and tenants' representatives was the government plan for laying the foundation of the bill that they contemplated introducing as a government measure later on. The tenants' representatives, who, in the then position of the land question, with prices falling and the third revision term looming in the distance, had all the trumps in their hands, were hopelessly outmanœuvred by the landlord section.

The question to be discussed was largely a financial[Pg 261] one, but still the tenants had not a man of financial ability at the board. It is true the members of the conference were nominated, and not selected by their respective sides, though afterwards, for reasons easily understood, the nominations were ratified by the parties concerned. But nominated by whom? By a Captain Shawe Taylor, a personage popular with all parties, but in this matter undoubtedly the agent of the government. The conference sat five times, and all through the proceedings the nationalist representatives were rubbing their hands with glee, for they thought the millennium had come.

The landlord party, on the other hand, were in nightly communication with the Castle. Treasury experts were drafted over to Dublin, and no stone was left unturned to secure for the landlords a measure which would satisfy the most exacting. They succeeded beyond their wildest dreams. On the 3d of January, 1903, the land conference issued its report. Clear-headed politicians saw at once that the tenants had played the game and lost. Every advantage or benefit that the landlord sought or claimed was secured to him by this treaty, as it was afterwards styled, in terms that could not be gainsaid. The tenants' clauses in the report were[Pg 262] mostly pious expressions of opinion, which were afterwards, when the Land Bill came to be drafted, brushed aside, or quietly ignored. But all was not yet lost.

The *Freeman's Journal*, under the able guidance of Mr. Thomas Sexton, in a series of powerful articles, reviewed the whole position. It boldly but temperately pointed out the defects in the conference report. It refused to shout with the crowd. It could not see that much was gained. It clearly saw that a great deal had been lost. The bill, a large and complicated measure of eighty-nine clauses, was shortly afterwards introduced. It was a great measure and aimed at the final settlement of the land question. And, indeed, such an end, devoutly to be wished, would certainly have been attained had the amendments pressed on the government during the passage of the bill by the organ of the tenants been accepted and embodied in the act.

Clause after clause was closely examined, and the defects exposed by Mr. Sexton in a series of articles, inspired if not actually written by him in the *Freeman*. He had done much service for Ireland in the past, but I doubt if his great abilities had ever been better applied than to the work of[Pg 263] examination, elucidation, and amendment of the Land Bill of 1903.

His criticisms culminated in the publication of a schedule of amendments which he claimed were necessary to the final settlement of the question.

It is worth while now putting them on record, for they have a true historical value. It is now seen in the working of the act, that the acceptance of some of the amendments contained in the schedule materially improved the bill, while the omission of the others explains the necessity for still further legislation on the subject.

The following is a summary of the amendments referred to:—

1. The rights of tenants under the Fair Rent Laws should be maintained intact.

2. No non-judicial tenant should be excluded from purchase by reason merely of his tenure. Caretakers of holdings of which they had previously been tenants should have the rights of tenants for the purpose of purchasing such holdings.

3. As a condition precedent to purchase, non-judicial rents and first term rents fixed or agreed upon down to the end of 1896 should be reduced to the average level, substantially of second term rents, and purchase should not be transacted in the[Pg 264] cases of non-judicial rents, or of such first term rents, except upon this basis.

4. The purchase system being voluntary, the compulsory limits of price in this bill should be struck out.

5. The aim of the system being to extinguish dual ownership and equal treatment being essential both as between past and future transactions, and also between the tenant who buys his holding and the landlord who buys back his land sold by him to the State, no rent charge should be reserved. Such a reservation would forever exclude the tenant from ownership, by erecting a new and perpetual system of landlordism in the place of the old.

6. The rate of interest on consols being now two and one-half per cent, the new guaranteed stock might be issued at two and one-half, instead of two and three-fourths as proposed, and by this means the decadal reductions, instead of being abolished as the bill provides, might be allowed at the rate of eight per cent; or, at the option of the purchaser, the period during which his annuity would be payable could be shortened by about ten years. If the annuity rate were three and one-half, the purchaser might be allowed to choose between decadal reductions at the rate of eleven per cent,[Pg 265] and a term of redemption shorter by nearly twenty years than that prescribed in the bill.

7. Sales of untenanted land, and, in particular, resales of demesne or other land to vendors, should be subject to the needs of migration, of enlarged holdings, and of making provision for evicted tenants, in the case of each estate or district, and no evicted farm should be resold to the vendor, or sold to a new tenant, if the evicted tenant, or his personal representative, is willing to become the purchaser.

8. The cost of improvement of estates and untenanted land, being charged to every purchaser and repaid by his annuity, should be provided for as part of the advances required for the purposes of this act, leaving the reserve fund available to the estates commissioners for cases of exceptional need.

9. It is necessary to maintain the existing satisfactory condition that the holding, or other land purchased, is to be sufficient security for the repayment of the advance.

10. The Purchase Aid Fund should be increased to not less than twenty millions; and distributed either in inverse ratio to the number of years' purchase in each case, or by a uniform grant of a fixed number of years' purchase to every selling landlord.

11. A term of years should be fixed in the bill,[Pg 266] on the expiration of which term the provisions for grants from the Purchase Aid Fund, resales to landlords, and distribution of purchase money free of cost should cease to operate.

12. The subject of sporting and mineral rights calls for clear provision dictated in the public interest, instead of the ambiguous, loose, and inconclusive proposals which appear in the bill.

13. It is requisite that the limit of advance to an evicted tenant be not less than the ordinary limits; also, that provision be made for restoring evicted tenants to their former holdings when vacant; for making arrangements to that end when the holdings are occupied; and for stocking the land.

14. The cramping restrictions imposed on the congested districts board, which have effectually prevented that body from dealing with the great agrarian evil of the West, would not be removed or substantially diminished by the meagre proposals of the bill; nor can the privations and miseries endured in the congested districts be sufficiently abated in any other way than by such a redistribution of grazing ranches as will provide the people of those districts with land enough to yield them the means of living. As the guarantee fund—now ample enough for every purpose—is henceforth to[Pg 267] apply alike to congested and other districts, and as advances for land purchase are seen to be free from risk, and special treatment is to be applied to congested estates throughout the country, it is evident that the time has come for a uniform system of land purchase, and that this is to be secured, either by investing the congested districts board, for all the purposes of land purchase in their particular areas, with powers corresponding to those of the estates commissioners, or else by giving the estates commissioners jurisdiction for land purchase in the congested districts, and authorizing the board to apply its income wholly to its various other objects of expenditure.

61

15. The proposals with regard to the Labourers' Acts are so trivial that they cannot be amended. The government should be asked to appoint a commission to inquire and report, this year, how the question may be adequately dealt with; and a bill directed seriously to that end should be passed into law next session.

The Irish Land Act, 1903, otherwise known as the Wyndham Act, from the name of the Irish chief secretary who introduced it, came into force on the 1st of November, 1903. This is not the place to set forth its provisions, but the principal advantages[Pg 268] which accrue to a selling landlord and a purchasing tenant availing of its provisions may be briefly stated. The entire purchase money agreed upon is paid to the landlord in cash. No part of the purchase money is retained as a guarantee deposit. For the purchase of a single holding the limitations of preceding acts are extended to £7000.

The vendor of an estate shall receive in addition to the purchase money from the tenants a bonus for his own immediate benefit. The landlord is enabled to sell his demesne, and repurchase it at a profit. The landlord may sell his estate direct to estate commissioners appointed by the act, or to the congested districts board, and these bodies are enabled to resell to the tenants after readjustment and partition of the holdings on the estate if necessary. Enlarged powers of investment of purchase money are conferred upon trustees. The principal advantages secured to the tenant are as follows: At the end of sixty-eight and one-half years, a tenant becomes owner in fee of his holding. As soon as the agreement to purchase is signed, he ceases to be liable for rent. He is enabled to repay the advance at the rate of three and one-fourth per cent of his purchase money. (Though the reduction of the annuity rate from four per cent under the previous[Pg 269] act to three and one-fourth per cent under the Wyndham Act is an undoubted advantage to a tenant, it is certainly to his disadvantage that the amount set aside towards the sinking fund should be reduced from one and one-fourth per cent and one per cent to one-half per cent.) In congested districts the land commission, or congested districts board, may purchase lands under certain conditions to enable them to deal with the problem of congestion.

The greatest blot on the measure is undoubtedly what is known as the "Zones." The act provides that if the price agreed upon between the parties allows a reduction of not less than ten per cent nor more than thirty per cent on a tenant's existing rent, in the case of a second term rent, and a reduction of not less than twenty per cent nor more than forty per cent in the case of a first term tenant, the bargain *must* be sanctioned by the commissioners without inquiring whether the land in question is security for the "advance."

The result of this provision is that tenants have been wheedled or cajoled into agreeing to bargains which they will find it difficult or impossible to keep. The price of land became artificially inflated, and the average of eighteen years' purchase paid for land[Pg 270] in Ireland under the previous Purchase Acts has been raised by five to seven years' purchase. It is essential that free bargaining should be restored if purchase is to proceed on sound economic lines. In spite of the efforts of the wisest of their leaders, the Irish tenantry are rushing into bargains under the Wyndham Act that may eventuate in dire consequences for themselves and for the country.

The importation of Canadian cattle when it comes will have a serious effect on the Irish produce market, and a further decline in produce prices may be expected.

Will the Irish tenant be then able to discharge his liability to the State and have sufficient margin for living? That is the question for the future. The answer to it alone can settle whether we have yet reached finality in the Irish Land Code.

Footnotes:
[1] Carlyle, Appendix, No. 17.
[2] See Lecky, II., 216 *et seq.*
[3] T. P. O'Connor, "The Parnell Movement," pp. 53, 54.